THE
ANNUNCIATION

A fictionalized work based on the Biblical
accounts of events surrounding the birth of Jesus
as recorded in the Gospels of Matthew and Luke

Dedication

This book is dedicated to the memory of my parents, Jacob Wesley and Dagny Zimmerli, who were married for seventy-two years until "death do us part," modeling what a husband and wife and marriage should be like.

This book is also dedicated to my wife, Mary, who has stood with me through good times and bad, richer and poorer, sickness and health for over 43 years.

CONTENTS

Acknowledgments

All Scripture quotations in this work are taken from the (NASB®) New American Standard Bible®, Copyright © 1960, 1971, 1977, 1995 by The Lockman Foundation. Used by permission. All rights reserved. lockman.org

The concept of the first-century Israelite house is from Logos Bible Software.

THE ANNUNCIATION

A fictionalized work based on the Biblical
accounts of events surrounding the Birth of Jesus
as recorded in the Gospels of Matthew and Luke

MICHAEL K. ZIMMERLI

Marshgrass Publishing

St. Marys, GA

MARSHGRASS PUBLISHING
ST. MARYS, GA

THE PHRASE, THE ANNUNCIATION, is most often applied to the angel's visitation of Mary, announcing to her that she would have a baby, the Son of God, and would call Him Jesus.

However, it is also used for other events, such as the angelic visitation to the aged priest, Zechariah, in the Holy Place of the Temple, the angelic appearance in a dream to Joseph, Mary's betrothed, to reassure him about taking Mary as his wife, and the unbridled proclamation and subsequent celebration of the Christ Child's birth by an angel army over the sheep fields on the Judean plains outside the City of David, Bethlehem.

Chapter One

A Stranger in the Temple

"And an angel of the Lord appeared to him, standing to the right of the altar of incense."

Luke 1:11

THE HAIRS ON THE back of Zechariah's neck stood up, a ringing began in his ears, and he almost needed to force himself to breathe. It was as though he was in the presence of something or someone with the power to erase his existence, but at the same time, he felt as insulated and comforted as when in his mother's arms as a small child.

Standing to the right side of the incense altar was a tall man dressed in robes so intensely white that they could have been woven from pure sunlight. There was something unusual about his countenance. Was he truly a man? If so, he was the first man Zechariah had ever met whose face shone like a mirror in the noon-day sun! Zechariah's head became light, and his aged knees felt as though they would give way. He quickly bowed before the shining apparition at the altar, then submitted to the feeling in his knees and stretched out with his face to the floor, completely prostrate.

"Do not be afraid, Zechariah. The LORD your God, Yahweh, is well pleased with you."

* * * *

"It has finally come to you, Zechariah."

The announcement didn't come from Israel's high priest but from one of the upper-level priests of their order, slightly beneath the High Priest.

Zechariah was a Temple priest descended from the tribe of Levi and the family of Aaron and a member of the priestly division of Abijah. There were 24 different divisions of priests, each serving in the Temple one week out of every half year.

When Zechariah was chosen for his task, there were 18,000 priests in Israel, 350 from the Abijah division alone. Only five of the 350 in Zechariah's division would typically be sent to the Temple in Jerusalem to fulfill their division's week of service for the next six months. There were many more priests than jobs, so they used lots to decide who did the various tasks during each division's week of service.

Casting lots—lots were small tiles or pieces of wood—was universally viewed as a form of divination by which the will of God was revealed, not gambling. Proverbs explains that God controls or manipulates the result of the casting of lots so that His will is manifest through the lot-taking.

"The lot is cast into the lap,
But its every decision is from the Lord."
Proverbs 16:33

Four lots were held each morning to determine who offered the burnt animal offering, the meal offering, who would burn the incense, and who maintained the candlestick in the Holy Place. Using lots prevented personal ego or favoritism from becoming a part of the selections.

There was only one afternoon lot, for the evening incense offering. With over 18,000 priests and Levites in Israel, offering incense was still considered a high privilege. It only came once in a lifetime since the chosen priest became ineligible for future lots until the other 18,000 priests of his division had received the privilege. It's easy to see why Zechariah had never been chosen to perform the incense ritual despite being well-known in the temple. Today, however, his name was chosen.

When told, Zechariah replied, "It is my joy to perform my priestly duty in the presence of Adonai."

He was glad to finally receive this once-in-a-lifetime opportunity and secretly glad he was not from the tribe of Levi, especially given the limitations outlined in the Book of Numbers.

"This is what applies to the Levites: from twenty-five years old and upward they shall enter to perform service in the work of the tent of meeting. But at the age of fifty years they shall retire from service in the work and not work anymore. They may, however, assist their brothers in the tent of meeting, to keep an obligation, but they themselves shall do no work. Thus you shall deal with the Levites concerning their obligations."

Numbers 8:24-26

The rules limiting Levitical (non-priestly) temple service to ages 25–50 were likely designed to ensure the men were old enough to have a certain level of maturity, wisdom, and sense of responsibility but also strong and healthy enough to perform the necessary physical labor. Levites aged fifty and over were not entirely excluded from service but were limited to less physically demanding tasks.

Unlike the Levites, priests were not retired at a certain age; they usually served until infirmity forced them out. Although Zechariah was over sixty, he was not considered elderly; many priests served into their eighties and even nineties.

Zechariah had been to the city of David many times, traveling from the hill country of Judea, where he and Elizabeth lived. But what a thrill! To finally be chosen to participate in the temple rituals. It would be a special occasion for him, an unrepeatable honor. Zechariah knew his time in Jerusalem was appointed by God. The whole process of the supervisor's fingers searching among the hundreds of pieces of wood in the box and finally selecting the one piece with Zechariah's name on it was all directed by God. The Lord had chosen him to come to the temple this year. And Zechariah knew it.

There were no windows in the holy place, so lamps were lit, wicks were trimmed, and oil was poured into the lamp's reservoirs each morning and evening. The sacred incense was burned each morning and evening according to a ritual passed from Yahweh to Moses and Aaron. Only the appointed priests were permitted to do these things. As outlined in Exodus 30, the incense was to be burned perpetually, just as God is infinite, without beginning or end.

"You shall put this altar in front of the veil that is near the ark of the testimony, in front of the mercy seat that is over the ark of the testimony, where I will meet with you. Aaron shall burn fragrant incense on it; he shall burn it every morning when he trims the lamps. When Aaron

trims the lamps at twilight, he shall burn incense. There shall be perpetual incense before the Lord throughout your generations."

Exodus 30:6–8

Even the recipe for the incense had been the same for hundreds of years, handed down to the priestly tribes from Moses.

Then the Lord said to Moses, "Take for yourself spices, stacte and onycha and galbanum, spices with pure frankincense; there shall be an equal part of each. With it you shall make incense, a perfume, the work of a perfumer, salted, pure, and holy. You shall beat some of it very fine, and put part of it before the testimony in the tent of meeting where I will meet with you; it shall be most holy to you. The incense which you shall make, you shall not make in the same proportions for yourselves; it shall be holy to you for the LORD. Whoever shall make any like it, to use as perfume, shall be cut off from his people. And he made the holy anointing oil and the pure, fragrant incense of spices, the work of a perfumer."

Exodus 30:34–38; 37:29

Only the High Priest could enter the Holy of Holies. The priest who offered the incense offering went in as far as the Holy Place, an outer chamber separated from the Holy of Holies by a thick curtain that stretched from ceiling to floor. The incense offering occurred in that outer room. According to Exodus 30:6, the altar of incense was placed right in front of the thick curtain separating the Holy Place from the Holy of Holies.

When Zechariah approached the incense altar, he would be as close to the presence of God as a man could be. Only the High Priest ever came closer to God's presence than Zechariah would be when he fulfilled his priestly duties. No other spot in the Holy Place was as close to God as this altar reserved for the perpetual burning of incense each morning and evening.

The priest presenting the morning incense offering stirred the coals from the previous day's offerings into fresh flame, yet another task chosen by lot. The priest chosen for the evening incense offering – Zechariah, in this case – would take the incense from a bowl, put it on the burning coals, and scatter it, raising clouds of smoke. The sight of the smoke going up from the Holy Place was a signal for the many worshipers gathered outside to pray.

Zechariah loved being a priest and looked forward to every opportunity to feel the nearness of God whenever he was within the Temple. For Zechariah, being chosen to burn the incense was not a "job" or just another part of his duties. He had been a priest for many years, but the feeling that came over him when standing inside the Holy Place never lost its newness. Unlike some priests in the Temple, Zechariah was upright in the sight of God, blamelessly observing all the LORD's commandments and regulations.

Not that his fellow priestly brethren had become jaded or turned from the path of righteousness. Oh, no, nothing as severe as that. It was just something he could hear in their chanting or see in their eyes: the slight boredom that can accompany any repetitious job, even one you loved. But Zechariah looked forward to each day and being able to serve the LORD in any way He saw fit to use him. Today, it was to complete a duty for which he had waited many years to hear his name called.

Zechariah was to enter the Holy Place alone, bearing the golden censer. He would be given a sign that he should spread the incense over the coals. As the incense kindled and a cloud of fragrance arose from the altar, the prayer of the worshipers outside would rise into the presence of God: altogether, it was a beautiful worship experience.

As Zechariah entered the Temple and approached the altar of incense, he breathed a personal, silent prayer that the LORD would accept him in His presence and give him a glimpse of the grandeur of His countenance. Zechariah lifted his head from his prayer and scattered the incense over the coals, using the censer he carried to spread the fragrant powder.

In the courtyard, the priests and the people had reverently moved back from the altar. They were prostrate before the LORD, offering unspoken prayer and thanksgiving for God's mercies, provision, and deliverance, along with petitions for blessing and peace. A cloud of smoke from the incense began forming and moving upward in the Holy Place.

Zechariah waited until he was sure that the incense was burning well and would have bowed down in prayer and reverently left the Holy Place, except he was suddenly aware that something was out of place in the chamber, a totally unexpected sensation.

The hairs on the back of Zechariah's neck stood up, a ringing began in his ears, and he almost needed to force himself to breathe. It was as though he was in the presence of something or someone with the power to erase his existence, but at the same time, he felt as insulated and comforted as when in his mother's arms as a small child. The ringing assaulting his ears changed to a sound like a rushing wind, except it seemed to carry his name with it. He was certainly getting much more than he had bargained for with this duty!

His eyes swept around the room. He had the uncomfortable sensation that someone was watching him, but no one was behind him in the Temple. There couldn't be; he was alone in this room. Turning back toward the altar again, he jumped in alarm, dropping the censer with a loud clatter, scattering the incense across the floor. As large as the temple was and as deep within it as Zechariah was, no one would hear the sound of the dropped brass censer. Even if they did, they couldn't identify it from all the other sounds emanating inside the temple from so many fervent worshipers.

Standing to the right side of the incense altar was a tall man dressed in robes so intensely white that they could have been woven from pure sunlight. There was something unusual about his countenance. Was he truly a man? If so, he was the first man Zechariah had ever met whose face shone like a mirror in the noon-day sun! Zechariah's head became light, and his aged knees felt as though they would give way. He quickly bowed before the shining apparition at the altar, then submitted to the feeling in his knees and stretched out with his face to the floor, completely prostrate.

"Do not be afraid, Zechariah. The LORD your God, Yahweh, is well pleased with you."

The voice that rolled out of this being was deep and rich, as smooth as the best-strained honey. It sounded as though it were no stranger to laughter yet was imbued with a ring of authority that caused Zechariah to remain prostrate on the floor. For some reason, the word "holy" leaped unbidden into his mind along with the words of Isaiah the prophet when he told of seeing the LORD sitting on a throne. Isaiah had cried,

---

"Woe is me, for I am ruined! because I am a man of unclean lips, and I live among a people of unclean lips; for my eyes have seen the King, the LORD of hosts."

Isaiah 6:5

For the briefest of seconds, the face of Zechariah's wife, Elizabeth, flashed through his mind; just as fleetingly, he wondered if he would ever see her again.

Like her husband, Elizabeth was descended from the family of Aaron, the priestly brother of Moses, who had led the Israelites out of Egypt. And, like her husband, Elizabeth observed all of the LORD's commandments and regulations. For many years after she and Zechariah had married, she had wondered what she was doing—or had done—wrong in God's sight, what sin she had committed that had caused Him to turn a deaf ear to her prayers for a child.

When her childbearing years had passed, she had finally accepted what she had known in her heart for a long time: she was barren and would never be able to give her husband a son. More than once, she had offered to leave Zechariah if that was his desire, setting him free to marry again and have a family.

He always laughed at her offer, saying, "Who would want to marry an old priest? We're no fun, what with all our prayers and rituals. Besides, what would a new woman and I talk about? No, my wife, it's *supposed* to be you and me. We have a history together, you and me. Let no man put asunder what God has put together, for it *was* God Himself who put us together, my dear wife. We were meant to be together, whether with children or alone, just the two of us. We are still *meant* to be together for a purpose."

Zechariah had laughed inwardly many times at the irony of the meaning of his name: 'Yahweh remembers.' For so long, he had felt Yahweh was utterly unaware of his existence and desire for a family. How could Yahweh remember him if He wasn't even aware of his existence?

The being before him was speaking again in his rich, smooth, baritone voice. "Do not be afraid, Zechariah. I mean you no harm. The LORD your God is smiling upon you today."

Dimly, he thought he heard the murmurings of the worshipers outside the Holy Place, thanking God for accepting their prayers as they rose on the smoke of the incense. The worshipers and other priests were oblivious to the fact that Zechariah was in mortal danger here, standing face-to-face with a creature who could surely snuff out his life as easily as Zechariah extinguished the evening lamp before going to sleep. Actually, 'face-to-face' was a bit of a misstatement, given Zechariah's current position on his knees with his nose to the Temple floor.

Chancing a glance at the being in the Temple with him, the old priest tilted his white-haired head and peeked across the room. The creature definitely had a male face framed by long, flowing hair that shone like gold against the pure white of his robes. Zechariah saw something even more unexpected than finding this creature or person within the Temple: it – or he – was grinning. In fact, it almost looked like he was trying to stifle a laugh!

"You may stand, Zechariah. I am not the LORD Most High, that you should cast yourself prostrate in my presence. I am His messenger. And today, I have a very special message for you." The angel paused, then added, "Do you need help getting up?"

"I think I'll just sit here for a minute if you don't mind," Zechariah replied, slowly rolling into a sitting position and rubbing his aching knees. "You ... *don't* mind, do you?"

"I am a messenger, and here is the message I was sent to deliver. Your prayers have been heard, Zechariah. Your wife, Elizabeth, will bear you a son, and you are to name him John. He will be a joy and delight to you, and many will rejoice because of his birth, for he will be great in the sight of the LORD. He is never to take wine or other fermented drink, and he will be filled with the Holy Spirit, even from birth. He will bring many of the people of Israel back to the LORD, their God. He will turn the hearts of the fathers to their children, and because of him, those who are rebellious will accept the wisdom of the godly. And why? To get the people ready for the coming of the Messiah."

For a moment, Zechariah just sat there on the Temple floor, taking in the words of this wondrous being. He was trying to understand what he had said, but he had stopped listening closely after the phrase "… will bear you a son."

He, Zechariah, would be a father after all these years? His faithful wife, Elizabeth, would finally give him what she had longed for since she was just a young girl? But she was no longer a young girl, and he was no longer a young man. How could this be possible? Elizabeth was well past her childbearing years.

Clearing his throat, Zechariah eyed the tall, robed figure. Summoning up his courage and doing his best to force down the fear that lurked in the back of his mind, the old priest said, "How can I be sure of this?"

The question seemed reasonable enough, and he felt it needed to be asked. After all, he was a priest chosen by God to communicate with His people. Now, he needed God to communicate with him. "I am an old man," Zechariah continued, "and my wife is well along in years. This kind of thing doesn't happen."

A hint of sadness crossed the face of the angel like a flicker of a shadow. Turning his back to Zechariah, he walked around the altar and said, "I am Gabriel, an angel of the LORD God. I stand in the presence of God, and I have been sent to speak to you and to tell you this good news. "

He paused briefly, and his voice became harder as he continued, "But because you questioned the message God gave you – because you did not believe my words, *His* words through my mouth, words which will come true at their proper time – because you did not believe, you will be silent and unable to speak until the day all that I have told you comes to pass."

His voice softened slightly, the steely edge replaced by the original silky smoothness, "And it will happen, Zechariah, just as I told you. God has spoken."

At the angel's words, Zechariah started to beg forgiveness, but no words passed his lips. He tried again, but only a barely audible "snick" of his lips parting reached his ears. Lowering his head, tears began to flow down his cheeks and onto his chest. His throat ached and burned with sadness, but no sound came forth. He swallowed against the lump in his throat and tried again to speak.

Nothing.

It was just as the angel had said. Zechariah was utterly bereft of voice. When he lifted his head again, the angel was gone. He glanced around the room, but he could tell without looking that he was gone. The powerful feeling of God's presence had vanished, leaving the room and Zechariah empty.

He thought again of Elizabeth, and it felt like a knife stabbed through his heart. Silent tears fell anew from his eyes, and his shoulders jumped up and down with soundless sobs.

Locked within his mind were the words she had longed to hear throughout their long marriage, and he had no way of releasing them from his mind. After so many years of disappointment and bearing the hushed whispers behind her back, she would have a baby, a boy. The message of Gabriel – *an angel of God!* – was locked behind his lips. Having no physical voice left to curse himself, he chided himself repeatedly inside his head for being a foolish, unbelieving old man.

The Annunciation

Chapter Two

A Quiet Reunion

"For nothing will be impossible with God."
Luke 1:37

OUTSIDE THE TEMPLE, THE other priests and worshippers were becoming concerned about Zechariah. He had been inside the Temple far longer than expected, even for an old priest. Sometimes, the older priests took longer to perform their assigned tasks, but Zechariah was taking far too long.

A murmur began running through the crowd. Priests began huddling together, quietly but earnestly consulting each other over what to do in this situation. This delay was highly unusual, and the priests did not know how to react. None of them were anxious to enter the Temple if something supernatural was taking place.

On the Day of Atonement, the high priest entered the Holy of Holies wearing a robe with bells on the hem. As long as the bells sounded, everyone knew he was all right. Although it was not prescribed in the Pentateuch, the first five books or scrolls of God's Word, it had become common practice to attach a silken cord to the ankle of the priest chosen to enter the inner sanctum. If the Spirit of the LORD should overcome a priest, the other priests could pull him out.

Zechariah did not have a lifeline. His duties did not require him to go beyond the outer room of the Temple. Those on the outside would simply have to wait until he came out. Most priests mumbled the same phrase to each other as they waited: What could have happened to Zechariah? But no one had an answer.

Inside the Holy Place, Zechariah imagined the buzz of the crowd outside as they speculated about what had transpired inside and slowly realized that he, Zechariah, was probably the cause of the commotion. The crowd was exceptionally large this season, as was the number of priests gathered in the city. They would need a good explanation. Well, he had one! He just couldn't *tell* them!

What a disappointment that he couldn't proclaim the good news to them! He and Elizabeth were finally going to become parents! At their age! It was an obvious sign that God was smiling on them, rewarding them for following His commandments all these years.

For years, they had quietly endured the pity of others, people whispering among themselves how God must undoubtedly be punishing the couple for some hidden, unknown transgression. Elizabeth's pregnancy would be their vindication! No more whispers or pitying looks! But … he could not tell them.

He swallowed and coughed, trying to clear his throat, but nothing came out, not even a croak or whisper. If he could whisper his good news, that would be wonderful, but somehow, the angel had removed even that possibility.

Even in his despair, Zechariah recognized the irony of the situation. How some would laugh at his condition: a priest unable to talk! There was hardly anything a priest liked better than the sound of his own voice as he expounded on God's will. But this loss of communication was no laughing matter to Zechariah. The angel had given him the most marvelous news, but because he had questioned the truth of it, he was unable to relate his good fortune to his fellow priests, to say nothing of the thousands of worshippers gathered outside. Or even his wife. *His wife!*

More than all the others he longed to tell her the news. The angel had said to him that many people would rejoice at the birth of their son. He, Zechariah, the father of this child, would be unable to rejoice with the others, all because he had not believed what the angel had said without questioning. It was not unlike the ancient story of Abraham and Sarah.

Sarah had laughed when told she would become a mother late in life. God had scolded her for laughing.

"But He did not take away her ability to talk!" Zechariah thought to himself.

The angel of the LORD had taken away Zechariah's ability to speak just when he had unbelievable news to tell. Nor would he be able to speak until the child was born …

Another terrible thought went through Zechariah's mind: as far as he knew, Elizabeth had not yet conceived. This silence could last for years! And then, despite his distress, he chuckled inwardly, *"It might take that long just to get Elizabeth to believe this amazing message!"*

Taking a deep breath, Zechariah began to pull himself together, picking up the censer where he had dropped it and gathering his legs beneath him. He thought about why he was in the Holy Place today. When the people saw the smoke rising from the Temple, it was supposed to symbolize their prayers rising to God, that his prayers had been heard. The thought shot through him again: *he was going to have a son!*

Slowly rising to his feet, Zechariah turned and glanced around the room once more. He wondered if he would ever feel the same in the temple. An angel from God with a personal message for him! His throat ached with the desire to shout praises to God for honoring him by making him part of his plan for Israel's salvation.

The angel had told him his son would be *great* in the sight of God and would turn many of Israel's people back to their God. He would be a part of God's plan for fulfilling the prophecies. The prophet Malachi said that God would send a *special one* to turn the hearts of the fathers to their children. The angel had said Zechariah's son would be that *special one,* chosen to make ready the way for the Messiah.

As Zechariah emerged from the inner room, the sight of a large contingent of anxious priests from his order greeted him. Behind them were the thousands of worshippers who had come to pray at the Temple as the incense was burned. The buzz and murmurs of the crowd had subsided entirely. Instead, they were hushed, all eyes fixed on this white-haired priest emerging long overdue from the inner room. They were waiting for him to say something, to explain his tardiness. All Zechariah could do was point to his throat and move his mouth so they would understand that he had become mute. He knew this would not hold the crowd long, so he lifted his hands skyward and gestured up, hoping they would understand that he meant God. Then he fluttered his fingers as he brought down his hands – angel wings? Gabriel had no wings that he had seen. Zechariah thought to himself, then pointed to his throat and open mouth again. He repeated his motions, and his message began to sink in. Zechariah had been visited by God while in the inner room and struck mute. Someone murmured to someone else, and they ran to get something to write with.

As the initial explanation passed back through the worshippers, there were shouts of joy. It didn't matter that they didn't know what the LORD had told Zechariah. It was only important that Yahweh had visited while they were here. In a way, they shared Zechariah's good fortune. At last, the people became satisfied with the story passing through the crowd and slowly dispersed. Zechariah and the other priests could resume an appearance of normalcy, even though only Zechariah knew how abnormal the situation truly was. He mutely decided he would not relate the whole story until he could do so in his own voice. Since he had completed his priestly duties and was slightly impaired by his inability to speak, Zechariah began his trip back home. He would have to write out his story for Elizabeth, but it was all he could do.

His wife was glad to see him, as she always was when he returned from performing his role as a Temple priest. She was cooking when he entered their house.

"Ah, Zechariah! You are home early! I am glad. I'll make a little more lamb, and there'll be plenty for the two of us. I trust all went well at the Temple. Were there many pilgrims among the regulars? Who was chosen to enter the Holy Place?" She paused. "Zechariah? Are you all right?"

He gestured at his throat, as he had done for the priests at the Temple.

"You can't talk? Oh, my! Did you sleep near a draft or sing and shout too much? And did your loss give the other priests cause for great rejoicing?" She smiled as she teased him. Then, seeing his serious expression, she asked, "Does it hurt?"

He shook his head. He made writing motions, and she immediately went to get a tablet and stylus for him to write with. He thought to himself, *'Where do I begin? How will I convince her I haven't gone mad? What if she doesn't believe? No. The angel said <u>she</u> would bear me a son. That means she <u>will</u> believe.'*

She returned with the writing supplies and gave them to him.

He began to write: *There was an unexpected visitor at Temple …*

Elizabeth did believe, and soon, she conceived. She and Zechariah praised God for his blessing, she with words and song, and he with silent prayers and adorations. For five months, she hid herself away, taking joy in her condition and meditating about the things the angel had told Zechariah. 'He shall be called John,' which means the 'LORD is gracious.'

"He is, indeed," she thought to herself.

The Annunciation

Chapter Three

An Unexpected Visitor

"Now in the sixth month the angel Gabriel was sent from God to a city in Galilee called Nazareth."

Luke 1:26

SHE SHUT THE DOOR tightly behind her before running to the window. Looking out, she scanned the street for the face of the man who had been following her. Seeing only the familiar faces of neighbors, she slumped onto the hard, wooden bench under the window. She was aware of her ragged breath and the sound of her pounding heart beating in her ears. Forcing herself to stand again, she turned and looked out the window for any sign of the man. The street was nearly empty now.

Taking a deep breath, Mary sat down on the bench again and clasped her trembling hands in her lap. Perhaps she was mistaken. Maybe she was letting her imagination run away with her. Sitting beneath the window, she heard the normal sounds of everyday neighborhood commerce, and her breath began to even out; her heart slowed down and became less audible in her ears, and her hands no longer shook. She told herself she was being a silly girl. She could feel the redness of her face and knew it was not only from running.

Nazareth was a small town, but there were no other towns or larger cities nearby, and as an isolated town, it was sometimes a rough place. People did get robbed, raped, and even murdered. Still, the neighborhood where Mary and her family lived was a safe, family-oriented area. Here, people didn't hide in their homes, huddled together against attacks by lawless gangs. This neighborhood watched out for its own. Mary knew all her neighbors, and they knew her and her family.

Rising to her feet, she smoothed her windblown hair, glanced out the window one final time, and breathed a deep sigh. She was home now, and even if a stranger had been in the marketplace, she was safe here.

She crossed the floor, her bare feet whispering against the well-worn mats that barely managed to cover the sandy soil they hid. Checking the coals in the rude clay oven, she began mixing the flour, water, and oil to make the flatbread that would be the main course of her evening meal. She chewed slowly on some dates while she kneaded the dough, enjoying their sweetness and letting her thoughts wander. Soon, she would be married, cooking for her man and, if Yahweh willed it, for her family.

Her thoughts carried her back to that afternoon when she had stopped by Joseph's shop. She loved to visit him there, surrounded by the tangy aroma of the fragrant wood shavings covering the floor. His face and hands were the color of bronze, tanned by many days under the hot sun. He was a carpenter, and a good one. Unlike other shopkeepers, Joseph's trade allowed him to work outside for much of the time. His arms rippled with each movement they made, betraying the strength of the muscles hidden under the skin, a byproduct of the rigors of his profession.

Joseph was older than Mary. For a long while, the feel of wood beneath his hands as he shaped it and the time spent with other craftsmen like himself had been enough for him. But as he grew older, he longed for the companionship a wife and family would provide. Joseph wanted to be more than a single-line entry in his family's genealogy. He wanted to raise a family, share his love for the wood, and pass along the secrets of working with wood. He desired to share another kind of love with a woman who understood him and wanted the same simple things he did. A woman like Mary.

They were both descended from noble families but so far removed that they could just as easily be descended from any family down the block. If you went further back, Joseph was descended from kings and Mary from lawgivers.

Both of them were strong in their beliefs, to the point of almost being old-fashioned. And, in the old-fashioned way, their wedding night would be the first time they would be truly completely alone. For now, there were always chaperones – aunts, uncles, and cousins – quietly vigilant in the background whenever the two were together. When Mary visited Joseph at his shop, other workers and customers were always around.

Mary was startled and jumped, her mind rushing back to her surroundings. Her hands paused their methodical kneading of the flatbread dough. The shadows on the wall had grown longer as the sun began to slip beneath the horizon; she hadn't noticed the room become dim. But it wasn't the dimness of the room or the dough in her hands that brought her back so abruptly. It was the sound of her name being spoken, not from outside or on the other side of the door but from within this room.

"Mary."

The voice was deep and rich, with a warmth like the golden color of the sturdy oak planks Joseph worked with. But it was not Joseph's voice nor the voice of any relative or neighbor. *The man she had seen in the marketplace!*

He had been following her, and now he was here, she thought, hiding in the shadows while she daydreamed. Dropping the lump of dough into the bowl, she began to edge away from the voice and the stranger speaking from the room's darkness. She needed to reach the door and escape. Her ears strained to pick up any sounds that might betray the stranger's movements in the growing dimness. Her pounding heartbeat filled her ears again, coupled with a raspy noise she realized was her breathing. If she could reach the door, she would run to Joseph and his strong arms that could deal with wild beasts and strangers alike.

"Do not be afraid, Mary. I have not come here to harm you."

Something about the voice made it seem to come from inside her head instead of across the room. It seemed to wrap itself around her with unseen arms, but not the dangerous, suffocating grasp like a man who had too much strong drink might grab an attractive girl he'd been eyeing all evening. The voice was like a comforting, enfolding embrace, as a father encircles a daughter in his arms after she bursts into his bedroom during a thunderstorm in the middle of the night. Mary's eyes were opened wide as she searched the corners of the darkness for the source of the voice.

"Calm your trembling soul, Mary, for I bring greetings to you from the LORD. You have found favor in His sight."

Though the words pierced the armor of her fright, they also brought Mary an entirely different sort of fear. She was an ordinary girl, betrothed to an ordinary man, destined to have an ordinary family and an ordinary marriage. The LORD Most High was singling her out? For what purpose? She had seen others supposedly chosen by God.

Those "chosen ones" lived alone in caves in the wilderness, subsisting on insects and rainwater, feared by children and derided by adults. Crazy old men and women, living a lonely existence, shunned by family and friends, listening to voices others never heard, shouting warnings of repentance to the townspeople. Was that the destiny the LORD had chosen for her? Was she to lose Joseph and the family they both wanted? Her heart began to ache with the thought, and tears stung her eyes and blurred her vision.

"Do not be afraid, Mary. You have found favor with God. A remarkable journey is to be yours and Joseph's."

This stranger knew of Joseph, then! He must have seen her at his carpenter's shop. But if what he said was true, she would not lose Joseph.

Finding her voice and taking strength from her thoughts of her beloved husband-to-be, Mary said, "Show yourself to me. Are you the stranger I saw today in the marketplace? Did you follow me? How do I know that what you tell me is from God Himself? What proof can you give?"

Mary turned her head at the sound of cloth rustling and gave a small gasp as the person belonging to the voice stepped from the shadows into the last fading rays of light streaming through the small window. He was tall and appeared very muscular under his cloak, with shoulders even broader than Joseph's, who could carry more upon his shoulders than most men. But the stranger's face gave her the most surprise, for it was the most handsome face she had ever seen.

Long, flowing hair the color of spun gold cascaded down over his broad shoulders, framing a face that seemed young but held a pair of eyes that seemed as ageless as the stars that shone brightly in the night sky over the mountains. The room grew even darker as the sun sank below the earth's rim, but she could still see the man's face clearly, for it seemed to generate a light of its own.

"Who are you?" Mary asked softly through trembling lips.

In response to her question, the tall, muscular man shrugged his broad shoulders, causing the cloak to fall to the floor, revealing robes whiter than the sun when it burned high over the marketplace at midday. Involuntarily, Mary's hand went to her mouth to stifle whatever sound was trying to escape. As the man smiled broadly at Mary, her knees began to give way, and everything changed to black. Mary knew that the man in front of her — not a man! — this "being" was not like her. He was not of this world at all! As the darkness began to wash over her, an impossible explanation came to her: the stranger was an angel!

49

Chapter Four

A Remarkable Announcement

"Behold, a virgin will be with child and bear a son, and she will call His name Immanuel."

Isaiah 7:14

Mary opened her eyes and looked up into the most handsome face she had ever seen, a face more handsome than any other man's on earth because this face belonged to someone who was not *of* this earth. He was an angel! Everything that had happened (could it have been just minutes ago?) came flooding back into her mind, threatening to cause her to swoon again.

Sitting up, trying to clear her mind that overflowed with questions, she said apprehensively, "What do you want from me?"

The angel smiled, and the entire room seemed bathed in a pure white light. "As I was saying," he replied in that voice so rich and comforting. "You have found favor with God."

"Why would the LORD God take notice of me? I am only a young girl with no special talents to offer Him." The questions teeming inside her were beginning to escape, and she struggled to maintain control.

"He sees inside you and knows your heart, Mary." The angel smiled as though he could see inside her heart, too, and knew the jumble of emotions and questions imprisoned there. "He hears your prayers, watches your footsteps, and sees what you see. He has been observing you since before you were even born, and He is pleased. And because He is pleased, He has sent me to tell you some great news."

Again, Mary thought of Joseph and how much she would miss him if the LORD needed her to live in the wilderness. "I am prepared to do what my LORD asks of me," she said, and she was. What she was not ready for was the message the angel had come to deliver.

"You will be with child and give birth to a son, and you are to give him the name Jesus. He will be great and will be called the Son of the Most High. The LORD God will give him the throne of his father David, and he will reign over the house of Jacob forever; his kingdom will never end."

Mary sat silently for a moment, taking in the words the angel had spoken. All the questions that had crowded her head a minute ago had vanished, replaced by ... nothing. She could not think. It was hard enough for Mary to remain in the presence of this being who was both terrifying and awe-inspiring at the same time. Part of her wanted to run from him, while another part wanted to remain, to soak up the holy aura he radiated. Slowly, she began to put his words in order, and the first concept she grasped had to do with her having a baby. Words began to tumble from her mouth as she again found her voice.

"Joseph and I are to have a son? A baby boy? Joseph will be so happy! He has spoken to me of how he wants several sons he can teach his craft to, who could take over when he gets older!"

The angel was smiling as he put a finger on Mary's lips and gave a gentle shake of his head.

"I said, YOU will be with child and give birth to a son. My message was for you. I was not sent to carry these same glad tidings to your betrothed. I am not privy to all the LORD's plans. I am only a messenger. My name is Gabriel. The LORD sent me to tell you that YOU will have a baby boy, and His name is to be Jesus."

Ordinarily, the firstborn son was named after the father in Jewish custom. To give the child a different name invited questions, at the very least, derision and accusations of questionable lineage at worst.

"This is not to be Joseph's child? But we are betrothed!" The questions began to pour forth from Mary. "I am to be Joseph's wife soon. Surely, he must be the father of my children. I have known no other man. I am still a virgin! If God sees my heart, then

He knows what I say is true. And, if I am not to be wed to Joseph, then to who?"

Gabriel took her hand gently and looked at her with those ageless eyes, eyes that had watched the history of man unfold.

"Do you not believe that the God of Israel, Adonai, the LORD of creation, can do anything, whether possible by man's laws or not? He brought the twelve tribes out of slavery in Egypt. He caused the walls of Jericho to fall and the mouths of the lions to remain closed when Daniel was cast into their midst, and He granted Sampson the power to conquer his enemies though shackled and blinded. He created the entire world and the stars above with a thought. It was He who filled the earth and skies with all manner of creatures, flooded it when it became corrupt, yet still loved it and its people enough to start afresh. Do you not believe He can do anything He wishes?"

Mary had grown up with the prophets' teachings and had heard her people's history since before she could walk. Her faith in God was unshakable.

"I do believe," was all she said in reply.

"The Holy Spirit will come upon you, and the power of the Most High will overshadow you," the angel explained. "All that He is will be joined with your seed, but without the taint of human sin. He will become truly human. Thus, the Holy One you will give birth to will be called the Son of God."

"I am to give birth to the Son of El Shaddai?" Mary exclaimed. The room began to spin, and she was afraid she would faint again. Then she felt a gentle but firm squeeze of her hand, which the angel was still holding.

"Put your head down and breathe slowly," he said. "The words of the LORD are often overpowering. What you are feeling is the strength of pure truth."

With her head down, Mary could not see the broad grin on the angel's face as he held her hand and waited for her to assimilate the knowledge he had imparted to her.

"Am I...?" Mary stopped, struggling to string her thoughts together. She tried again. "Am I still to wed Joseph?"

Gabriel said nothing.

Raising her head and looking him full in the face, Mary asked him again, "Will Joseph and I still be able to get married?"

"There are things which were not made known to me," he said again.

Mary lowered her eyes from his. The angel continued to speak.

"But take heart, Mary. Ours is a God of love and order. You have found favor in His sight, as has Joseph, who you know to be an upright man of great faith. Would it not be unseemly for the Son of God to be born into a scandalous situation? Would not the arduous road He must walk be made that much harder if he were labeled a bastard? Does not our God rejoice and bless the union of man and woman when they merge into husband and wife? When Adam wandered alone among the beasts of the new world, did not God in His infinite wisdom give him Eve as a companion and helpmeet?"

Pausing for just a moment to allow his words to sink in, Gabriel continued, "I cannot tell you what decision Joseph will make. All I can say is trust in the wisdom of our God."

Mary turned her head and let her hand slip from the angel's grasp. So much to think about! How could she possibly understand the implications of what she had been told by this being of light from above? She was no scholar from the Temple, well studied and versed in the teachings and history of her people, her religion.

Yes, she knew the commandments and kept them, but she was only a young woman, accustomed to deferring to elders and scholars for answers to important matters. How could God have chosen her?

Out of all the women in the world, how could He have noticed her? Only her?

"There is one other thing our LORD tells me to pass on to you."

"More?" she thought to herself. *"I haven't been able to make sense of what I've already been told!"* But instead, she said nothing and merely nodded her head.

"Your aunt Elizabeth is going to have a child as well."

Mary couldn't keep the words in. "But how is that possible? She is an elderly woman, long past childbearing age, and has been barren all her life! She and Zechariah have prayed for children every day of their marriage."

The angel stood up. She hadn't even noticed that he had been sitting beside her since she first fainted upon realizing he was an angel. Now, he rose and stood over her, his presence filling the small room. Yet, despite his size, she no longer feared him.

This man who was not a man fixed her eyes with his and said, "She who has been called barren is now in her sixth month. You see, Mary, it is for her even as it shall be for you: nothing is impossible with God." Reaching out a hand to her, he helped her to her feet.

His words echoed in her mind, and she knew the truth of them: nothing is impossible with our God.

"I am the LORD's servant," Mary answered. "May it be to me as you have said."

She turned and walked a few steps away, looking slowly around the darkened room as she continued to contemplate the impossible news she had received. The glow that had filled the room was gone, and she did not need to turn around to know that the angel had vanished. Lighting a candle, she sat down near the oven and picked up her flatbread dough again.

For a long while, she sat there, holding the dough and thinking about what she had been told, marveling at the incredible news. Her feelings were running between astonishment, amazement, and joy. Not only would she bear a son - the Son of God! - but her aunt Elizabeth was to have a child as well.

Truly, nothing is impossible for the LORD Most High!

The Annunciation

Chapter Five

A Sudden Stirring

> *"Thus the LORD has dealt with me, in the days when He looked on me, to take away my reproach among people."*
>
> Luke 1:25

ELIZABETH LEANED BACK AND placed her hands on her belly. She knew she was pregnant. Now. When she first began to notice the changes in her body, she was uncertain whether it was complications from the change of life or something worse that was wrong with her. After a time, though, it became apparent to her that she was finally going to have a baby.

Other women her age were doting on grandchildren while she was about to have her first child! She had asked herself many times how it could be happening now, but she always arrived at the same answer: The Almighty Father has a sense of humor! For Him to decide at this stage of her life to bless her with a child was beyond her comprehension.

The loose, flowing garments she wore hid her growing abdomen when her husband came home from performing his priestly duties. Zechariah, being even older than she, was no longer as observant of the changes in her shape as he had been when they were younger.

How she loved this man whom God sent to be her soul mate. All the years they had longed to share their love with children. How many times had they had their hopes dashed?

Now, their lives were turned upside down, but he had no voice – he had been rendered mute. He understood she was pregnant but could not get any words to come out.

For her part, she understood that *something* had happened to him at the Temple six months ago, but she didn't know all the details. What she did know sounded too fantastic to be correct. But through it all, they continued to praise Almighty God and trust in His wisdom.

Standing near the low parapet at the edge of the flat roof of their home, Elizabeth saw a small figure off in the distance on the road below: a girl. Something about the girl's clothes and gait struck a chord in her mind. Could this be her niece, Mary, from Nazareth? Why would she come here now, when she was betrothed to Joseph, the carpenter? Had there been some trouble?

She wondered if Mary would notice her condition. She was probably coming with news about her upcoming wedding to Joseph. She was only a young girl and would probably not notice her aunt's recent physical changes. Besides, who would expect someone as old as Elizabeth to be with child? *No one!* At the thought, the corners of her mouth turned up, forming a smile while her eyes sparkled with the joy she felt. She could scarcely believe it herself!

Looking again at the figure walking on the dusty road, Elizabeth could see that it was Mary. It suddenly became crucial for her to see Mary and to stand in her presence. It was as though her heart was trying to pull her across the flat rooftop and down the stairs. She was barely aware of walking to the steps and descending to the room below. She felt a compelling urge to speak with her niece, to stand in her presence.

Elizabeth tried to be calm, but something within her pushed her to move faster, faster! She hurried to the door, nearly tripping over the mat on the floor. She decided to meet Mary in the street and walk with her.

Instead, upon opening the door, Elizabeth found herself face-to-face with an out-of-breath Mary. She must have run the last few yards to Elizabeth's house. Gasping for air as a little trickle of sweat slid down from one eyebrow, the young woman panted, "Elizabeth! I have heard the most incredible news! And you'll never guess who told me!"

Elizabeth gasped, for her world changed again at the sound of Mary's voice. The pounding in her chest suddenly felt like it spread outward until her whole body joined her heart, beating with an inner power. Elizabeth focused solely on her niece.

As Elizabeth heard her niece's voice, the child in her womb stirred as though trying to jump up and down. At the flutter of movement within her, Elizabeth also sensed a presence as though someone else was standing with the two women. It was a warm, secure presence, not at all threatening. It was as though the two kinswomen were wrapped in a blanket of the softest wool, and somehow, Elizabeth knew it was the presence of God – His Spirit. But that was not all she knew. Suddenly, she knew what had brought Mary to her door.

Elizabeth pulled the younger girl toward her, grasping Mary's hands in her own. Looking deeply into Mary's eyes, Elizabeth said in a voice she could hardly control, "Blessed are you among women! And blessed is the child that you will bear."

She realized she was squeezing Mary's hands tightly and loosened her grip as she continued, her voice intense but almost a whisper. "Why should this great thing happen to me, that the mother of my LORD comes to visit me? For as soon as I heard your voice, the baby within me jumped with gladness! Blessed are you for believing that what God has told you will be accomplished!"

The two women stood in the doorway for a moment, basking in a soft warmth that did not come from the sun overhead but from the presence they both felt surrounding them. They gazed into each other's eyes, and Mary's hand slowly reached out and paused just short of touching Elizabeth's stomach. Elizabeth smiled and nodded, and Mary placed her hand on her aunt's swollen stomach. The child within lurched a few more times, then relaxed, but Mary kept her hand where she had placed it. A long moment passed before she took her hand away. Elizabeth led Mary wordlessly into the house.

Sitting together, knee to knee, neither spoke for a long time, afraid of losing the wonder of the moment or causing the presence of the LORD to withdraw. Elizabeth finally broke the silence.

"How did you know? About me, I mean. You obviously knew. But *how* did you know?"

Mary told her about the angel's visit, the message he gave her, and how he told her of Elizabeth's pregnancy. As she spoke, Elizabeth could do little more than nod and listen, wondering what it must be like to stand in the physical presence of something or someone who communes with God directly, a creature not of this world. Zechariah knew, and Mary knew, but Elizabeth could only guess. She suspected it was similar to the feeling she had at Mary's arrival.

Then Mary said, "My soul praises the LORD, and my spirit rejoices in God my Savior, for He has remembered me, His lowly servant! From now on all generations will call me blessed because of the great things the Mighty God has done for me. His name is holy. From one generation to another He shows mercy to those who honor Him. He has stretched out His mighty arm to those who think of themselves as mighty, and he has scattered them about; He has brought down kings from their thrones. Yet, at the same time, He has lifted up the lowly and fed the hungry while sending the rich away empty-handed. He has kept the promise He made to our ancestors, and has come to the aid of His servant Israel. He said He would be merciful to Abraham and his descendants forever, and He has not forgotten His promise."

For a while, the two women continued to sit quietly, two women chosen by God for roles neither had sought. After a time, Mary's youth and curiosity pushed their way to the surface, and she began to ask Elizabeth about her pregnancy, questions any ordinary young girl on the eve of marriage would ask. And Elizabeth answered them as best she could, much of her knowledge being secondhand since this was her first pregnancy.

The wonder of what had passed between them remained in the back of her mind, along with the knowledge that this newly pregnant young girl would never have a completely normal life again.

Chapter Six

Confession and Confusion

"…before they came together, she was found to be with child by the Holy Spirit."

Matthew 1:18

Joseph TOSSED AND TURNED, unable to get comfortable on his bed. He had been up most of the night, unable to fall asleep. His mind wouldn't shut down. He kept seeing the scene repeatedly in his head.

Mary had come to see him—the girl who had captured his heart and given him hope of having a life of companionship instead of a life of loneliness. After three months apart while she visited her Aunt Elizabeth, Mary had returned to him. But she was not the same girl who had left town three months earlier.

When she came into his shop, she seemed even quieter than usual. He wanted to believe she was just tired from her journey, but he soon found out that was not the case. She seemed tentative, as though she was unsure of what she was doing, the way she had been when their betrothal began nearly a year ago. They had known each other for some time, as was typical. Not as long as those who were "engaged" when they were three or four years old, but long enough. Their espousal was the last step before their actual marriage.

In many people's eyes, indeed, even legally, they were already married. If the groom died during the espousal period, the bride was considered a widowed virgin. If a couple chose to break up at this time, they needed to sign a bill of divorce. But Joseph and Mary were serious about their future together. Even though some couples married for money, power, or convenience, Joseph and Mary were genuinely in love.

She stood in the corner near the doorway with a handful of wood shavings that must have been very interesting, judging by the intensity with which she was staring at them. She was silent for a few minutes, then closed her eyes, took a deep breath, and raised her head.

"Joseph, we have to talk."

It was those words all husbands dread, a phrase Joseph already knew meant Mary was serious. Usually, Mary talked, and Joseph listened. But when she said they needed to talk, it was to be a serious discussion. So, Joseph put down his tools, brushed the sawdust from his apron, took a rag, wiped his brow, and sat down on a small stool near Mary. He was aware that the noise in his shop had quieted as their ever-present, nearly invisible chaperones went about their business more quietly, ostensibly to allow Mary and Joseph to hear each other but also to be sure they could hear what the couple was saying to each other.

Mary did not come any closer but no longer stared at the wood shavings. Her gaze was now fixed upon Joseph with the same intensity she had shown the wood shavings. It was clear to her that he had no idea what she was about to say. In truth, she had no idea what she was about to say. Though it had been three months since the day the angel Gabriel had visited her, it seemed like it had been only hours before. The changes her body had begun to undergo told her it was no dream. She really was pregnant, even though she had never been with a man.

"The Holy Spirit will come upon you, and the power of the Most High will overshadow you; and for that reason the holy Child shall be called the Son of God."

The same power of God that was with Moses had come to her, Mary, from the little town of Nazareth. How could she tell Joseph that God had picked her out from all the others in the world? How could she make him believe? Her body told her it was true, but who or what would tell Joseph?

"Joseph, we have both heard the words of the prophets many times, which speak of the coming of the messiah."

Joseph nodded. He could not imagine where this was going or why she had such a serious countenance.

She continued, "The prophet Isaiah said a virgin would conceive and give birth to a son, and his name shall be Immanuel – God is with us. Do you believe the prophecies, Joseph?"

Someone must have said something that tested Mary's faith. Perhaps the priest, Zechariah, who is married to her Aunt Elizabeth. He could have confused her. He knew much, having been a priest his entire adult life and having studied the prophets' scrolls for so many years. But what could he have said to upset Mary?

"I believe the prophets, Mary," Joseph answered. "You know that. I may not always understand them, but I believe they are of God and worthy of study. Why do you ask?"

"But do you believe this particular prophesy? And do you believe ..." She paused and swallowed and, in swallowing, encountered a lump in her throat. Her eyes began to sting. *No! Not now!* She chastised herself silently. She needed to be strong. If she started to cry, he would think she was a silly little girl, unable to keep her emotions in check, maybe too young to get married.

She bit her lip sharply until it almost bled and then tried speaking again. "Do you believe me when I say that I love you and look forward to being your wife, giving you sons and daughters, and growing old with you?"

Joseph could see his beloved Mary was engaged in a serious internal war. She was apparently dealing with something very upsetting. He would have to talk with Zechariah sometime and ask him not to upset Mary in the future. He stood up from the stool and took a step toward Mary.

She responded with a step backward, like an elaborate dance, edging closer to the open doorway. Joseph stopped moving.

Holding out his arms to her, he said, "Of course I believe you. Do you not believe me when I tell you how much I look forward to keeping you busy with babies and laundry and mending and cooking?" He was trying to calm her, to let her know he would try to make everything all right again for her, but she stayed where she was.

"Do you believe me, Joseph, when I say I would never lie to you? That I will always trust you and always be trustworthy for you? Since our engagement, I have only had eyes for you. And since our betrothal, I have counted the days until you will come and take me for your bride. So, do you believe me when I tell you that I am still a ... virgin? That I have never been with a man? That I have no desire for any other man?"

Now, a small tear escaped from the corner of her eye. She turned her head and dabbed at it quickly with the hem of her sleeve. Joseph tried to take another step closer, but Mary held up her hand. As small as she was and as big and strong as he was, she could still stop him in his tracks with one delicate hand.

"You must answer my questions, Joseph." Her eyes burning, her vision of him blurred through salty tears, she looked him in the face and asked again, "Do you believe I am still a virgin?"

"Has someone implied that you are not?" He could feel the fire of righteous anger growing in his chest. Had someone accused her of something improper, and she wanted to be sure he had not heard? He was unsure how it fit with her questions about the prophets, but that was unimportant.

"Who has accused you? Not I, and I am the one who matters most. If I thought it was so, I would have to fill out the bill of divorce. Who has accused you?"

According to Jewish law, when a man decided to dissolve a betrothal instead of finalizing the marriage, he issued a document called a bill of divorce, known commonly and simply as a "get."

"No one has accused me, my love. Nor do I accuse you."

"Then what is the meaning of your questions?" he asked.

"It is not an accusation, but it will soon be obvious to all, especially you. Though it will not be the truth they think they know, it will be a form of truth nonetheless."

She looked down, which caused her nose to run from the tears so close to cascading down her cheeks. Sniffling a bit as she took in a breath, she lifted her head and said, "Joseph, I am with child."

He felt as though someone had struck him with a mallet on the top of his head. His vision became a mix of reds and blacks. There was a ringing in his ears and a tingling in his fingers. He took a small step back and bumped into the stool he had been sitting on. Confused, he stared down at the crude seat and, without thinking, sat down on it again, feeling a need to get off his feet.

"How...?" He could not fathom what she had just said to him.

"I don't know exactly how. I only know that I am … yet I am still a virgin, and I am still – and always have been – true to you. I have never been with a man, keeping myself pure for you, to give myself fully to you on our wedding day. An angel visited me, and he told me Yahweh had chosen me, and I would become pregnant. The LORD'S Spirit would come upon me."

"Mary, I may not be the smartest, most handsome, or well-traveled man, but I do know where babies come from. I can hear the words you are saying, but in light of what you just told me, they don't make any sense. How can a woman be pregnant and no man be involved? It doesn't just not happen; it *cannot* happen."

Still sitting on the stool, a piece he had made with his own two hands with tools he had also crafted, he continued, "God made man and woman in such a way that you need both types to make a baby. If what you say is true, then I must not be in the same world anymore."

Mary started to speak, but this time, it was Joseph who held up a hand, silencing her and forcing her to listen to what he had to say.

"If what you say is true, how can the other things you told me be true? How can you stand there and say you love me and want to marry me and have my children, and yet in the same breath say you are already pregnant?"

Trying to prevent his mind from conjuring up pictures of the scenarios that could have resulted in this conversation, he plunged ahead, "You tell me this *news* after being away for three months! What am I supposed to say? What can I possibly think? What am I supposed to do?"

As Joseph spoke, Mary slowly slid down against the wall behind her until she was sitting, and she wrapped her arms around her legs. She rocked gently, holding herself. *He doesn't believe it. How could he? What I asked of him was too much.*

In her mind, doubts began to flare like red splotches on a whitewashed wall. The angel had not said she and Joseph would stay together after this. He had been clear; he had warned her. He said *she* would have a baby, not *they* would have a baby.

Running his hands through his hair and down his cheeks over his beard, Joseph turned and took a few steps toward the piece of wood he had been working on before Mary came. He picked up the plane he had been using and placed it against the wood.

This was something normal. This felt the way it should, the way it always did, the way he expected it to. He stood, stretched out, and pulled the plane back against the wood, creating a curl that fell to the floor and joined its brothers. *This* was what he knew.

Without looking at her, he said, "I'll take care of the bill of divorce. I know someone who can help get it done quietly so your name isn't ruined. You can go away to Elizabeth's and have the baby. Then, after a time, when you come back – if you want to come back – you can find someone else who doesn't know … your history."

As he uttered the words 'your history,' Mary let out a tiny sob. Joseph felt his heart tearing in two, but there was no other way. How could he marry her now?

She was damaged goods. Even if a Roman soldier had raped her on the road to Elizabeth's, she could have told him, and they would have worked through it. That sort of thing happened on a regular basis since the Roman army had come to occupy the territory. The soldiers considered it to be open season when it came to the local women.

But this story of Mary's? Pregnant but still a virgin? And by a Spirit? Whether a child by a Roman thug or … anyone else was believable. But by a … *thing*? That just wasn't possible. The next question that came to his mind was whether he could raise someone else's bastard son or daughter as his own.

The child would always be a reminder to him. He didn't know if he could truly love it.

When Joseph turned around, Mary was gone. Rather than leaving to look for her, he returned to his woodworking, but it no longer comforted or interested him. He sat down on the stool. After a long while, he gazed around the room. He wondered when their chaperones had left. What had they heard? It didn't matter, though, because there was only one course of action for Joseph now. He would see about the divorce tomorrow. There was no sense in waiting.

Chapter Seven

Visions in the Night

But when he had considered this, behold, an angel of the Lord appeared to him in a dream, saying, "Joseph, son of David, do not be afraid to take Mary as your wife...

Matthew 1:20

"JOSEPH, I AM WITH child. I don't know exactly how. I only know that I am, but I am still a virgin, and I am still true to you. I have never been with a man, keeping myself pure for you, to give myself to you on our wedding day. An angel visited me. He said the Spirit of the LORD would come upon me."

That had been this afternoon. Now he lay on his bed, trying to sleep, to escape the day's turmoil and the "situation." Finally, deep in the night, sleep stole quietly into his room to provide some relief.

But as Joseph slept, his dreams took him back to his shop. In his dream, the comfortable work of shaping wood and the familiar rhythms with the tools of his chosen trade all seemed as natural as ever. But something was different. He didn't feel alone in the shop. He could sense a presence as if someone were watching him. In his dream, Joseph looked around his shop to see who was in his private place.

He saw a figure sitting on his little stool near the door, just watching Joseph work.

"Is there something I can do for you?" Dream Joseph asked the man, for the figure was more manly than feminine. "Is there something you need here?"

The man continued sitting on Joseph's stool. In his dream, Joseph took a step or two toward the man. "I asked you a question," he said.

The man didn't move, but a voice came from his direction, deep and warm. "Nice wood. What kind of tree did it come from?"

Relieved that the man was finally talking, Joseph answered, "It is nice. It's oak. Good and strong. It'll last for years and still look pretty when we're old and withered."

A smile flickered across the stranger's face at Joseph's comment about the wood and their growing old and withered. "And where did the oak tree come from?" he asked.

Joseph gave a smile of his own and replied, "The mighty oak comes from the lowly acorn, of course. Anyone knows that."

"And where did the acorn come from?" the man of many questions asked.

"Why, from another oak tree, I guess," Joseph answered.

"But where did the first oak tree come from?" the stranger wanted to know.

"From Yahweh, the LORD God," Joseph told him. "The God of my father and his father and his father before him. The God of King David, King Solomon, the God of Abraham, Isaac, and Jacob, the God of Moses and Aaron, the God of Noah who survived the Great Flood. The same God who created Adam, the first man on earth."

The man remained seated on the stool. The shadows cloaked him enough that his features were mostly hidden from Joseph. "The LORD God Almighty created an oak tree without needing a male tree and a female tree? He created a self-sustaining tree? As long as there have been oaks, there have been acorns. Without acorns, there would be no more oaks. And yet there was a time when God decided to make an oak tree, and He did it without an acorn or even a squirrel to bury the acorn."

Joseph answered without thinking, "Yahweh can do anything. It was He who created the entire world and all the creatures and plants upon its surface, all the fish in the seas, and the birds in the air. He created Father Adam from a handful of clay and our mother Eve from a rib He took from Adam's side."

"And is this what you believe, Joseph? Search your heart for the answer to my question. Your future may depend on your answer."

Joseph could feel the stranger's eyes probing deeply into his soul, even though his eyes were hidden from Joseph. He had not even noticed that the man had called him by name, though Joseph had not mentioned it. Many people knew of Joseph of Nazareth, the carpenter.

"Who are you, stranger? I have been polite and respectful even though you came into my shop without so much as a knock on the door. Why do you ask me about my beliefs? Perhaps you should seek out a Temple priest if you have more questions. They have been trained to answer questions like the ones you ask. I am but a humble carpenter. You have come to the right place if you need something built or fixed."

"Oh, I am in the right place, Joseph of Nazareth, descendent of King David, carpenter and betrothed of Mary, she who revealed to you the Good News from Yahweh to the people of the world."

Mary! Who was this stranger? Joseph felt his chest tighten at the mention of Mary's name. Even in his dream, the memory of her announcement caused his heart to ache.

Joseph took another step toward the stranger, squaring his stance for whatever might come next, and asked - no, almost shouted - "What do you know of Mary? And how do you know what she told me?"

The man took in Joseph's stance, which would have intimidated any other man. But the stranger continued calmly, comfortably sitting on the stool, unmoved by Joseph's movements and words.

"You say you believe God can make a tree from nothing and a man from clay. You believe the world was created by the LORD Most High, including the vast seas and the limitless skies overhead. And you believe these things without ever having seen God or heard His voice. Yet, when the woman you have held in your arms and spoken with for untold hours on end, a woman you have come to love and trust, who has never lied to you, when she tells you that God has chosen her to be the vessel for man's salvation, you choose not to believe. Your thoughts immediately turn base and crude. Your thoughts immediately accused her: *'Surely, she is lying. She MUST have lain with some man!'* You do her a great disservice, Joseph."

The man stood now, and Joseph was forced to look up into the stranger's face, for he was a good head taller than Joseph and broader across the shoulders as well. Joseph's questions had vanished along with his voice. Not that it would have done him any good if he could speak.

The stranger continued to talk, sweeping past Joseph with a rustle of his robe to stand next to the piece of wood Joseph had been working on. He put his hand on the partially-formed piece of timber, caressing it gently, feeling its rough spots and smooth.

"She is not lying, Joseph. She is still a virgin. And, yes, she *is* with child. But this is no child of man. He is to be the Son of God, the one the prophets spoke of so long ago. Joseph, do not be afraid to take Mary as your wife. The child within her womb was conceived by the Holy Spirit. You shall name Him Jesus, for He shall save His people from their sins."

Questions swirled in Joseph's brain, asking why Mary had been chosen, why her when she was promised to him? But all he could manage to get past his lips was a feeble, "But … why …?"

"It is all done to fulfill the prophecy. Did you not listen when Mary asked if you believed in what the prophet Isaiah said? Is your head as hard as this piece of oak? Isaiah said it would happen this way. Did you think he was just talking to hear himself talk? He was passing on the Word of God so your people would keep watch and wait, trusting in the steadfast goodness of the LORD."

"Are you … a prophet? Or are you a priest?" Joseph asked, finally finding his voice. "What is your name, stranger? Who – or what – are you? You have opened my heart and shown me my anguish, but you have also said there is a way out of despair."

"Who am I? My name is not important. Let's just say I am a messenger." And the tall stranger smiled. "The God who created the earth, the sea, the sky, and even the oak tree wanted me to tell you that you are still Mary's betrothed. Even as she has been chosen, so *you* have also been selected for this unique role. It was not chance that drew you and Mary together. You will have the task of being the earthly father of the Son of God and a hand in raising Him – just as you would any child.

"Mary needs your strength, support, and understanding, but most of all, your love. Rise now from your slumber and go to her. Take her as your wife. Be happy together. Love God and watch and marvel as He pours out His love on all mankind through the fruit of her womb. It will be a good life together for you and Mary, Joseph.

"I must go now, and you must awake. You need to get married!"

Joseph opened his eyes and found himself in his bed, alone in his home.

Tears began to well from his eyes as he remembered the dream and all the turmoil that had occurred yesterday. He allowed the tears to roll down his face for a moment, then wiped his face with one hand, sat up, and began to dress.

Today was his wedding day!

Chapter Eight

Nissuin

"For I hate divorce," says the LORD, the God of Israel…"

Malachi 2:16

THE JEWISH MARRIAGE PROCESS occurs in two distinct parts: *kiddushin* (commonly translated as betrothal, usually a year-long period) and *nissuin* (the actual marriage). Kiddushin reflects the sanctity of the marital relation and sets aside the woman to be the wife of a particular man and no other. If the man were to die during the year of kiddushin, the woman would be called a virgin widow. The betrothal is a legally-binding relationship that requires a divorce to break.

Once the kiddushin is complete, the woman is legally the man's wife. Their relationship, created through the kiddushin, can only be dissolved by death or divorce. The spouses do not live together during the time of the kiddushin, though, and the obligations created by a marital relationship do not take effect until the nissuin.

In the same way that the couple's relationship can only be dissolved by death or divorce, if either partner commits adultery during the kiddushin stage, the result is the same as for any fully married couple.

Under the Law of Moses, adultery was punishable by stoning.

And Joseph her husband, being a righteous
man and not wanting to disgrace her, planned
to send her away secretly.
Matthew 1:19

The word, *nissuin*, comes from a word that means "elevation." The nissuin completes the process of marriage. The husband brings the wife into his home, and they begin their married life together.

"Then the LORD God said, "It is not good for
the man to be alone; I will make him a helper
suitable for him."
Genesis 2:18

Joseph was not sure where he would find Mary. Yesterday, he had suggested that she go back to Elizabeth's until she had given birth, but she had said nothing. He could not even remember when she had left his shop last night. *Last night? Had it only been a few hours?*

According to Jewish law, if a man decided to dissolve a kiddushin instead of finalizing the marriage, he issued a document called a *"sefer k'ritut"* – a scroll of cutting off – but known commonly and simply as a "get." Originally, the man wrote a bill of divorce, handed it to the woman, and sent her on her way. To prevent frivolous divorces, the rabbis added complex rules, from the document's language to its delivery to the acceptance by the woman. There was rarely any reason for the dissolution given in the document. It simply stated that the woman was free to marry another man.

If a man refused to give his estranged wife a get, she became an "agunah," a chained woman, unable to divorce according to Jewish law and thus unable to remarry.

Joseph had told Mary he would take care of everything. There would be no stoning, no public ridicule – at least not by him – just a quick and quiet release for both of them. Or so he thought yesterday afternoon.

"How similar to my previous vow to take care of her forever, yet so completely different!" he thought as he pulled on his tunic. When he told her he would take care of everything, he meant he would have the "get" written up, dissolving their betrothal, their kiddushin. But that was before he had had a

conversation with the visitor, an angel. He said Joseph had also been chosen to be involved with this miraculous baby she was carrying. After telling Joseph he needed to find Mary and take her as his wife, the man had simply vanished in his dream.

So now, Joseph *needed* to convince Mary that he still wanted to marry her. Joseph paused as he rushed around his room, getting ready to leave his shop to search for Mary. He stood quietly for a moment, letting his emotions and thoughts gather so he could sort them out in his mind.

"Do I want to marry her? Yes. Do I want to have a family with her? Yes. Can I love this ... child *she is carrying?"* He asked the questions in his mind and answered them, too, except for the last one. The first two questions were easy, the last one not nearly so.

Another question was going through his mind as well: had an angel actually visited him in his dreams, or was it just his mind helping him work through this quandary his heart wanted to avoid? Did it matter? He had decided to take Mary as his wife, and that conviction remained solid in the light of day. He needed to hang on to that conviction.

Finishing dressing and preparing quickly, Joseph left his house. He was in such a hurry that he had to rush a few steps back to kiss the mezuzah on the main doorpost. Joseph had decided to go to the home of Mary's parents. Hopefully, she had, too.

Before he had gone very far, though, Joseph slowed his frenzied gait. If Mary had gone home and told her parents the same story she had told him and his decision to seek a divorce – however quietly – there would be swift and possibly harsh consequences. Her "infidelity" would hurt her parents' standing in the community. They might simply have her and her bastard child shunned, or they might turn her out on the streets to fend for herself. Joseph could not let that happen. He increased his speed, needing to find Mary before she said anything to her parents.

Joseph found her in a grove of olive trees. She was sitting under a tree with her back against it, the grass tall and going to seed. The sun was streaming through the leaves, warm where it touched, whether on the face or shoulders.

He slowly approached Mary, unsure what reaction his presence would elicit. It had been less than a day since he told her he would take care of arranging a quiet divorce. Less than a day since he told her he didn't believe her story of an angel visiting her and revealing to her that she had been chosen to carry the yet-unborn Son of God. But that was before his own angel visit.

She didn't say anything when he came near. She didn't look up at him or indicate that she recognized his infringement upon her time in the sunshine under the trees. That was bad and good, but at least she hadn't run away from him or thrown things at him. She also wasn't crying, but her eyes were slightly puffy, indicating that she had been crying.

Joseph stepped over by the tree opposite where Mary was sitting and, turning to look directly at her, asked, "May I?"

Still not speaking, she gave an almost imperceptible nod. Joseph slid down the tree until he sat on the ground, his back against the tree. He sat quietly, looking at Mary and listening to what his heart was telling him. He had a feeling she was doing the same.

"What changed your mind?" she suddenly asked. She was looking at a stalk of tall grass she had plucked, not at him. It was as if she had asked the grass the question.

"What makes you think I've changed my mind?" Joseph replied.

The corners of Mary's mouth turned up slightly, barely perceptible, except Joseph had seen it many times before and recognized it. She had him.

"I was praying out here last night, and I felt like God was speaking to me," she said. "I didn't hear a voice, and an angel didn't visit me, but I got the impression in my spirit that God was speaking to me. He told me not to worry because you would come around. He said He had it all arranged, and it would happen just the way He planned it. I said it might help if you were visited by an angel, too."

Joseph could barely breathe. This woman was fearless, but she was right. She knew him well. He wondered if God knew what He was in for, choosing her as the mother of His Son.

Joseph told her about his dream and his need to find her this morning before she said anything to her parents.

Mary responded, "I knew God was going to work it all out; I just had to wait for Him to move you in the right direction. And He did."

Joseph stood and brushed the dirt from his cloak. He walked the few feet over to where Mary still sat. He reached a hand down to her, which she took. He helped her to stand to her feet.

"Are you ready to start this journey?" he asked.

Mary rubbed the slight roundness her belly had become.

"I've been walking on the road already. That's why I knew you'd find me here this morning. I knew God didn't make a mistake choosing you as the man to raise His Son. We've been handpicked to walk this journey together. You know what Ecclesiastes says about the strength of two…"

Joseph answered, "If one can overpower him who is alone, two can resist him."

They finished the verse together. "A cord of three strands is not quickly torn apart."

"You and I make two strands, but God makes it three," she continued. "And that's unbreakable."

"Are you ready to get married?" Joseph asked. "We'll go tell your parents that we need to move the wedding date up a bit."

Holding hands, they walked out of the olive grove.

Chapter Nine

An Army of Angels

---

*"This will be a sign for you: you will find a
baby wrapped in cloths and lying in a
manger."*

Luke 1:12

THE JUDEAN COUNTRYSIDE WAS clear and crisp that night. The sky was filled with stars, and a bright moon, making its slow march across the sky, rose over the hills, the moon's light reflecting off the herds of sheep huddled together.

"Abba?"

"Yes, Caleb?"

"Did you always want to be a shepherd?"

Caleb's father, Asher, poked the logs on the fire, sending up a flurry of sparks into the night sky. They both watched the sparks swirl for a second.

"I'm not sure 'want' is the right word, Caleb. I always *knew* I'd be a shepherd. It was never a question. My father was a shepherd, and his father before him. All my brothers are shepherds, like all the men in our family. Think about the men in the field tonight – Levi, Benjamin, Amnon, Nathan, Melech, and Reuben. All your uncles or cousins. None of us had any dreams of being something other than shepherds. Or, if they did, they put it away to be what they needed to be. Our family business is sheep herding."

Caleb sat quietly for a while.

"Abba?"

"Yes, Caleb?"

"What if I don't want to be a shepherd?"

Asher looked at his son's thirteen-year-old face reflecting the firelight. He enjoyed having his son working with him, but it meant answering questions like this one.

"No one wants to be a shepherd!"

Nathan's gruff voice came from a dark spot to one side of the fire. He was curled up, looking more like a pile of rags than someone sleeping. He sat up and moved a little closer to the fire.

"No one with half a brain wants to be a shepherd, Caleb, but it's just what we do. You heard your father – it's what your grandfather did and his father before him. It's also what his father did before him and his father before that. It's who we are. Shepherds. Smelly, dirty, ceremonially unclean shepherds. The lowest on the list. Well, not as low as Samaritans or lepers, but pretty low on the list."

"Or Roman soldiers," Asher added.

Nathan spat on the ground and cursed, "Roman dogs, you mean."

Asher gave a dark chuckle, then submitted one more group low on the list. "We're not as low as tax collectors. Not by a far sight."

"They're the worst of the worst," Nathan agreed. "They steal from everyone, including their own people."

"Abba, what's a tax collector?" Caleb asked.

Before Asher could answer, Nathan roared with laughter. "It doesn't matter, Caleb! We don't pay taxes, so we don't worry about it! Nobody comes out to the sheep pastures to collect from shepherds! Besides, we barely make anything to tax!"

"I don't want to be a shepherd, Uncle Nathan."

"Oh, you don't. Why not? Are you too good to be a shepherd?"

"That's not what I'm saying. I want to *own* the sheep I look after, not herd them for someone else."

"Why on earth would you want to have the headache of owning sheep? They're some of the stupidest creatures the LORD Most High created."

"That's not fair, Nathan," Asher interrupted. "And if the boy wants to have dreams, let him have dreams. King David was a shepherd. I'd say he turned out all right."

"King David was the exception to the rule, and you know it, brother." Nathan snorted in derision.

"Abba?" Caleb tried to get his father's attention.

"There are other options, Nathan. This isn't the old days. Boys have more chances to do other things now than they did in King David's time—"

"—Abba!"

"What is it, Caleb?"

"I think there's a fire. There's a bright light over there." Caleb pointed past the nearest edge of the herd, and there was indeed a glow, and it was steadily growing brighter.

Asher and Nathan stood to try to get a better look. Suddenly, as they watched, a man appeared, his face and robe shining like the sun reflected directly on him, but it was the middle of the night.

"Do not be afraid!" he called out.

Too late! Asher thought. He saw Nathan fall face down in the grass and dirt to his right. Grabbing Caleb, Asher pulled his son down to his knees; Asher ducked his own head, bowed low, and kept his face toward the ground while holding onto Caleb with one hand.

"I mean you no harm," the man announced. "I have a message for you."

"Please, lord," Asher said, his voice shaky, "we're merely shepherds. We just watch the sheep. That's all."

The man came closer, and Asher noticed that he carried no lamps, torches, or lanterns, yet a light blazed around him. It seemed to come from the man and reflect from his face at the same time.

"And an angel of the Lord suddenly stood before them, and the glory of the Lord shone around them…"

Luke 2:9

"I'm here to announce a great and joyful event that is meant for everybody worldwide: A Savior has been born tonight, in the town of King David – Bethlehem – a Savior who will be Messiah and Master. You and your brothers should go because He has come for all men, not just the priests, royalty, or Jews. He is the Savior for all mankind. You need to look for this: a baby in a stable, swaddled in a blanket, and lying in a feed trough."

The shining man stopped speaking and was silent for a few seconds. Asher started to lift his head to see if he was gone. Perhaps it had been a dream. Maybe he was sleeping right now!

The grassy plain suddenly blazed with light as though ten thousand torches had been lit. The light was as intense as the sun at noon in summer but without the heat.

Asher could see that it came from an army of men, glowing like the first man. The entire plain was covered with tall, broad-shouldered men in pure white robes. Without warning, they began praising God in unison:

"Glory to God in the highest,

And on earth peace among men with whom He is pleased."

Though they weren't singing, there was a rhythm to the words. Then they began repeating and echoing the words in smaller divisions, like a round. The hills echoed the voices back at this impossibly huge choir, amplifying the sound even more.

Their voices were so loud that Asher was sure he and his son and brother were about to die. He raised his head again slightly and saw that the sheep were still exactly as they had been before the multitude had arrived, quietly grazing.

The army of … angels? continued to praise God with their song, spoken and at times shouted, without a distinct melody yet always completely harmonious, voices blending with a counterpoint that shouldn't exist without a basic melody. Yet it went together seamlessly, inviting everyone who heard it to join their voice with the throng.

Asher was on his knees now, amazed that the sheep were not frightened, listening, watching, and wholly caught up in the words of this heavenly choir. He realized tears were streaming down his face, and his heart felt like it would burst with a joy he had never felt.

The first man, who had made the initial announcement, raised his hands high over his head, and the choir stopped, but the sound continued to roll over the Judean hillsides, echoing back their joyous song. As suddenly and silently as they had appeared, the army of angels vanished, the light gone, leaving only the bright moon overhead and the firelight to give the shepherds sight.

Asher sat on his haunches, and Caleb crawled to him and pulled his father's arm around himself. Nathan was lying on his belly, his head still down, his arms over his head protectively. Asher could hear the shouts of other shepherds running toward their fire, their hollering carrying across the short distance.

"What was that?"

"Who were they?"

"Have you ever heard anything like that?"

"Did you hear what they said about a Savior being born tonight in Bethlehem?"

Asher got to his feet, drawing Caleb up with him, keeping him under his arm beside him, like a mother hen shelters her brood.

"Of course, we heard him. He stood right in front of us and announced it to us," Asher replied.

"He stood in front of us," one of the other shepherds said.

"No, he stood in front of us," said another.

They ceased their random comments. They realized the message had been given to each of them, almost individually but somehow shared with all at the same time. As the other shepherds stepped within the firelight, Asher saw tracks down their cheeks where tears had flowed, and he knew his face looked the same.

Caleb was pulling at Asher's outer cloak. He looked down at his son and heard him say, "Abba? The angel said we should go and find the baby. I think he meant tonight."

They were only a couple of miles from Bethlehem. It would not be difficult to make their way to the town. The moon was bright, the distance short.

Bethlehem – the City of David, the Shepherd King, a small, humble town. Bethlehem Ephrathah, the prophet Micah, had called it.

> *"But as for you, Bethlehem Ephrathah, too little to be among the clans of Judah, from you One will go forth for Me to be ruler in Israel. His goings forth are from long ago, from the days of eternity."*
>
> *Micah 5:2*

As Asher looked at the other shepherds gathered around the fire, he realized he could see each man's face clearly. It was as though each man was holding a small hand lamp in front of their face, but without the flickering that a small flame would cause. They had been in the presence of men – no, angels – from heaven. Their light had been the glory of the Most High, reflected from their faces – just like Moses after he was on Mount Sinai to receive the Law. In the short time the shepherds had been with the angels, their faces now shared that glow, reflecting the glory of God Himself.

"We must go to Bethlehem," Asher said, raising his hand to silence his brothers and uncles. Tonight. Right now. The angel said we should go. Let us go and worship the Savior who has been born. Yohanan and Menahem are injured and have volunteered to stay with the sheep."

Caleb stretched up and whispered in his father's ear. Asher nodded and said, "We'll find him in a stable, lying in a feed trough. How many babies are lying in feed troughs in Bethlehem tonight, do you suppose?"

Without another word, they began to walk in the direction they knew Bethlehem lay, except Nathan. Asher turned back and hurried to his brother, who was finally standing after keeping his face buried in the sand and dirt during the encounter with the angels.

"Aren't you coming, Nathan?"

Nathan squatted beside the fire and used his staff to jostle the logs.

"Nathan?"

"No. I can't go. You go. And tell me about it when you come back. Take Caleb. He, of all of us, must see this Savior."

"But why, brother?"

"It's like the prophet Isaiah when he saw the Lord on his throne, high and lifted up. He cried, 'Woe is me, for I am ruined! Because I am a man of unclean lips, and I live among a people of unclean lips; for my eyes have seen the King, the Lord of hosts.' I am a man of unclean lips, Asher. I know this from seeing the army of angels who appeared here tonight. I don't think I could stand myself if I saw the Savior. I already know I am a sinner. Seeing the Savior wouldn't change that. I'll stay with the others and watch the herd. I am a shepherd, after all. That's what I do."

"Abba…" it was Caleb, calling to Asher.

Asher stepped forward, threw his arms around his brother, and held him tightly. He whispered, "I'll tell you all about it when we get back. And I'll tell the Savior you're being a good shepherd."

"Abba!"

Asher stepped back and released Nathan. There were tears on both their faces. Asher realized Nathan's face didn't have the same glow the other shepherds had, the residual effect of being in the presence of the heavenly beings. Nathan had hid his face on the ground rather than look at them and now, he was about to miss out on another blessing. But it was his choice.

"I'll tell him about you," Asher said as he turned to join Caleb and the others already hiking toward the town where a baby was waiting to meet them.

"He's a baby, Asher. Maybe I'll see him when he grows up. There's always time."

"You mean like there was time for our brothers Oren and Levi? You never know when your time is up, Nathan. If you have a chance to see the Savior promised since antiquity—and told to us by an army of angels!—you need to take it."

The two brothers stared at each other across the slight gulf, their faces illuminated by the flames of the campfire. After a short time, Nathan's shoulders relaxed, and he looked away from his younger brother.

"You're right, Asher. Let's go to Bethlehem. A baby can't be as scary as an army of angels, right? C'mon. Let's catch up to the others."

Caleb's plaintive call floated on the night air back to them. "Abba!"

"We're coming, Caleb!" Asher shouted. Then, in a softer voice heard only by the two brothers, he said, "We're both coming to meet the Savior."

The Annunciation

Chapter Ten

Divinity in a Diaper

"For today, in the city of David, there has been born for you a Savior, who is Christ the Lord. This will be a sign for you: you will find a baby wrapped in cloths and lying in a manger."

Luke 2:11–12

"ABBA? CAN WE REALLY just walk through the town in the middle of the night? And no one gets suspicious?"

"We do it all the time, Caleb. Except we're usually pushing a herd of sheep to take them to the other grazing grounds. We do it in the middle of the night so we don't inconvenience anyone," Asher answered his son. This was the first season Caleb had stayed out in the field with the men of his family, so he had many questions, especially about regular practices that the older, more experienced men took for granted.

"But we don't have any sheep with us now. What if someone asks us why we're walking through town?"

"We'll tell them to mind their own business!" Nathan answered gruffly.

"We'll tell them we're on a special mission for the King," Asher answered, nudging his brother with an elbow. "We'll tell them it's a mission of great urgency, and we're just passing quickly through town because it's the fastest route. Does that sound plausible, Nathan?"

"It sounds close enough to the truth to make people hurry back inside to their beds so we don't make them come along with us!" Nathan replied with a gruff chuckle.

"How will we know where to look for the Savior, Abba?" Caleb wanted to know. It was the same question Asher had been asking himself since arriving at the town's edge.

They were lucky this was Bethlehem, not Jerusalem, with all its special-purpose gates and guards standing watch all the time. Bethlehem was just a tiny rural town, well-acquainted with shepherds and sheep. Even though King David had come from Bethlehem, he and his whole family had been shepherds.

The lambs from Bethlehem served a special purpose: they were offered as sacrifices during the spring feast of Passover in Jerusalem. The gutters in the big city ran red with the blood of the lambs as priests offered sacrifices on the altars for the sins of the people. It was true that the lambs for sacrifice came at a premium price, but it was also true that the cost of penance rose accordingly in conjunction with the three major feasts: Passover in the spring, followed fifty days later by Shavuot or Pentecost, and the autumn feast of Sukkot or Booths, a harvesttime pilgrimage meant to remind Jews of the years they wandered in the desert on the way to the Promised Land.

In the spring and fall, the Judean hillsides were the nearest stockyards. Jewish shepherds raised sheep and prepared them for sacrifice, even though they were consistently ceremonially unclean. Being unclean went with the job: handling dirty animals and their dung and blood.

None of the shepherds in the field that night had ever taken part in the major feasts in Jerusalem, despite the requirement for Jewish men to attend as often as possible, at least once a year. Bringing the lambs apparently gave them special dispensation, but no one wanted to rub elbows with a shepherd anyway. As much as a shepherd may try to wash away the sheep odor, it always lingered, marking him as a shepherd and, therefore, more than likely unclean.

The older shepherds were used to passing through Bethlehem in the middle of the night, but they usually led a herd of sheep with them when they did. Going through Bethlehem was a shorter route than herding the sheep around the town's perimeter, so they simply went through the middle of town at night when no one cared.

The midnight dash through town worked well for townspeople and shepherds alike. It should also be noted that the shepherds felt equal disdain for the townspeople who couldn't see the value of the shepherds' work and saw them as the lowest of the low.

That night, the shepherds were not merely walking through town; they were looking for someone in particular. The angels had said they would find the Savior, the Messiah the Jewish nation had been praying centuries for, in the form of a baby born in Bethlehem and lying in a feed trough, a manger.

Most of the houses were two stories, consisting of several upper rooms for visitors and a lower main floor the family shared with the livestock. While an Israelite family's animals were allowed to roam and pasture outside during the day, they were gathered into the side stable room at night for protection and to take advantage of their body heat that would help warm the home during the cold season.

A typical Bethlehem home consisted of four to six modest rooms. On the bottom floor, there was an open 'courtyard' for cooking and working, a stable area for animals, a room for the family, and a room for storage. The upper floor had a main room with a side or utility room on each side of the main room with ladders leading to the flat roof. Family members often used the roof in the warm summer months for additional living and sleeping space. The houses were typically about 24 feet wide by 24 feet deep and 15 feet high.

When guests stayed with the host family, the guests generally stayed in the upper living room. Either because they had come too late or due to Mary's impending birth, Mary and Joseph stayed on the first floor with the family.

Recently, Caesar Augustus had called for a census to be taken, and people returned to where their roots were to be counted in the census. Anyone descended from King David came to Bethlehem, but many people in town were not related to the king at all. Distant cousins who hadn't seen each other in years – and people who had never been in Bethlehem in their lives – were coming to town to be counted in the census.

Joseph and Mary had come to Bethlehem to be counted since both were descended from King David and were, in fact, distant cousins. Joseph needed only to recite a portion of his lineage to find a welcoming face.

"I am Joseph, son of Jacob, son of Matthan, son of Eleazar, who was the son of Eliud."

His lineage opened doors in Bethlehem as easily as a key in a lock. The upper room was already full, but upon seeing Mary's advanced pregnancy, Joseph's distant cousins squeezed a little closer on the main floor to provide space for Joseph and Mary. The animals in the stable stalls were of no concern to anyone, especially not anyone who had just made a 90-mile trip.

Joseph's relatives welcomed the newlyweds as the extended family they were. When they arrived, Mary was nearly ready to deliver her baby and in no condition to make the trip back to Nazareth. The family insisted the young couple stay with them until after the baby was born. Joseph helped out by making things from wood and fixing things that had fallen into disrepair – tools, kitchen gadgets, toys, and even making a new stone feed trough, a manger, for the stable area. As he suspected they might be when he made his occupation known, his skills were soon in high demand in the neighborhood.

When Mary went into labor, Eliana – the woman of the house and one of Joseph's distant cousins – shooed all the males out of the lower level, sending them up the ladders to the upper room where the extended family was staying. Some of the men went outside to build a fire and share a few bottles of wine and tell stories about when their children were born.

A few of the men had protested, especially Eliana's husband, because almost everyone there had been around women giving birth before. But Eliana insisted, knowing it was Mary's first time. She offered to be a midwife for Mary, who was greatly relieved to have another woman with her, one who had been through the process several times herself and had helped numerous other women deliver. Several other women from the extended family stayed to offer support, stories, and on the off-chance that they might be needed for assistance or advice. With Joseph's help, they rigged up a birthstool for Mary, and then he was also banished from the women's domain.

At first, Mary was self-conscious about the situation with so many women in attendance, and she was confused by the device, but Eliana, as the midwife, told her that Hebrew women had been using birthstools for hundreds of years. It's mentioned in Exodus, in the story of Moses, when the new king of Egypt became nervous about the overwhelming number of Israelites.

"Then the king of Egypt spoke to the Hebrew midwives[…]; and he said, 'When you are helping the Hebrew women to give birth and see them upon the birthstool, if it

*is a son, then you shall put him to death; but
if it is a daughter, then she shall live.'"*
Exodus 1:15-16

"The Hebrew name for the birthing stool is 'double stones,'" Eliana explained to Mary, her history stories distracting the soon-to-be-mother from the pressure and discomfort she was feeling; it was an alien feeling for the young girl.

"The original birthstool was a pair of stones, set together in such a way that each stone supported each thigh while allowing a gap between them to aid the midwife in helping the mother to deliver."

Mary quickly discovered that the birthing stool made the contractions more productive, but in between, she could rest and gather her strength. During one of the pauses between contractions, she asked Eliana what her name meant.

"The first part is easy," she answered. "You know that el– means the LORD Almighty, as in Elohim. The other half – ana – means 'answered.' So together, they mean 'the LORD answered.' What do you think? Does it fit? My husband always says he should have asked, 'What was the question?' when we were introduced." Eliana laughed softly, a melodic sound that helped put Mary's fears at ease.

'God has answered,' Mary thought. *'He knew I would need help and support, and He answered my prayers. Surely He caused Caesar to need a census, bringing us to Bethlehem and Joseph's relatives' home and then letting me know He was here with me through the meaning of her name. God has answered! Indeed, He has!'*

Eliana continued talking, her voice soothing and calming. The other women were quiet spectators, available if needed.

"I have no daughters, only sons," Eliana said. "While many see me as blessed for providing my husband with sons, I have often wished for a daughter. In the short time you have been with us, Mary, I have grown fond of you. I know you are blessed by the LORD Most High. As your labor continues, I will sit behind you, and you can recline against me between contractions. It will be soon. I wanted to make sure you were aware."

Mary could feel another contraction building and would force her to give it all her attention in just a moment. "What do I need to do?" she asked, even as the contraction rolled over her body. She felt her stomach muscles tightening, and the cramping feeling went through her and down her back. She felt like her whole body was clenching. She gripped the sides of the birth stool and rocked slightly.

"Shh, not yet," Eliana said softly. "I'm here to help you through. I won't leave you here alone. It is written, "The LORD is the one who goes ahead of you; He will be with you. He will not fail you or forsake you. Do not fear or be dismayed" (Deuteronomy 31:8).

Mary took hold of the promise of God in her mind. The contraction was over soon, but longer than the last one. When it was over, she sagged, tired from the exertion.

"My hands will hold yours when the contractions come," Eliana explained, "and I will help you bear the pain. Your baby is coming soon. Perhaps God will bless you with a son."

"Yes, Mary answered tiredly. "It will be a boy."

"Lean back and rest against me," Eliana told her.

"What about Joseph?" Mary asked, suddenly concerned about her husband.

"This is not a place for men. He did well to stay as long as he did, but I could see the relief on his face when I shooed him from the house. Besides, according to the Law, he would become ceremonially unclean if he were involved. Don't worry, Mary. I promise you, he hasn't gone far. As soon as he hears his baby's cry, he'll be trying to break down the door to get to your side."

Time seemed to speed up and slow down, and Mary had no idea how much time had passed, but eventually, her baby was born. Whenever Mary felt the contractions seizing her body, Eliana would let her squeeze her hands tightly, leaning into Mary from behind. Mary got the mental picture of two mighty arms wrapped around her, but they weren't Eliana's. They were the arms of God. He was with her throughout the process, just as He had promised.

After Eliana had cleaned up the baby – yes, it was a boy – rubbing it with salt and gently rubbing olive oil all over his skin, they wrapped him in cloths. However, these were not ordinary blankets or towels Mary swaddled Jesus in. They weren't rags the young couple had brought from home or had scrounged from Eliana's during the weeks they had lived there. These were the same cloths used by the priests at the Temple to keep the lambs clean and free from blemishes as the lambs were prepared for sacrifice.

They were from the priest, Zechariah, and his wife, Elizabeth – Mary's relatives. Mary had stayed with them for three months while she was pregnant, and the cloths were a gift. Elizabeth had said, "I feel like I need to give you these cloths to wrap your baby in. The lamb who will one day take away the sins of the world."

As Mary fell into an exhausted but welcome sleep, Eliana laid the baby in the nearby manger Joseph had recently made for the livestock. Joseph soon came in and took the baby in his arms, and slipped outside with him. Eliana had warned her ahead of time that this is what men did. After the wife did all the work, the husband took both the child and the credit for bringing him into the world.

The Annunciation

Chapter Eleven

A Great Rejoicing

"When they had seen this, they made known the statement which had been told them about this Child. And all who heard it wondered at the things which were told them by the shepherds."
Luke 2:17-18

ASHER WAS MOVING FROM house to house, watching for signs of a new baby – exactly what signs those would be, he wasn't quite sure. He was mainly looking for a house with lights still lit at this late or early hour, depending on one's point of view. For the moment, Caleb was searching with his uncle Nathan.

Asher remembered when Caleb was born and his insatiable desire to suckle at all hours of the day or night. That was why he was watching for signs of someone being up and about during the third watch of the night.

Then he heard it: a man's voice, soft and low. It was coming from somewhere off to Asher's right, so he veered in that direction. He saw a dim light a couple of feet off the ground. When he got closer, he realized it was a lantern set on a rock. He could still hear the man's voice, soft and almost in a sing-song tone.

Asher finally saw the man's shape, silhouetted against the night sky, blocking the stars more than anything. Asher crept forward as softly and quietly as possible. When he was only about ten feet away, he could see that the man had a bundle in his arms. He spoke to the bundle, occasionally singing little snatches of songs that Asher recognized from when Caleb was a baby. The man was swaying from side to side, holding the bundle against his chest.

Asher knew it was a baby, but was it *the* baby? He watched the man interact with his child briefly, then, trying not to startle him, Asher softly cleared his throat. The man stopped swaying, but he didn't whip around to see who was behind him. He pulled the baby close and wrapped his cloak over the baby before turning around and facing whoever had interrupted this personal moment.

"Good morning, sir," Asher said softly. "And should I say congratulations, too? Is that a new lamb you have with you this night?"

The man stepped carefully forward toward Asher. He had pleasant features, and his expression showed no sign of animosity or danger. In fact, he was smiling from ear to ear.

"This is my son," the man said. "He was just born a little over an hour ago. We're staying with family, and the time came for Mary – she's my wife – to deliver. I left her sleeping and brought the baby out here to get to know him. I wanted to explain the world to him, how he came to be and to tell him his name."

As Joseph came near to Asher, he noticed the slight glow that still remained on the shepherd's face after his encounter with the angels and the glory of God that had shone so brightly on them.

"Are you a man, kind sir, or are you an … angel?" Joseph asked, tightening his grip on his precious bundle.

"I'm as much man as you are, sir. I'm just a shepherd from the grassy fields a short distance away. Why would you ask if I were an angel?"

With his free hand, Joseph made a circle around his face. "There's a faint glow about you."

"Ahh. Yes, I imagine there is." Asher remembered vividly the sound of the angels praising God, and he felt a sudden lump in his throat. He cleared his throat and said, "My brothers and I were visited tonight by a choir of angels, a veritable army of heaven's own, singing, 'Glory to God in the highest, And on earth peace among men with whom He is pleased.' It was like nothing I had ever heard. And do you know why they were singing? They told us that a baby had been born in Bethlehem, and he would be the Savior of the world. They said we should come to Bethlehem and see this Savior. And they said, this will be a sign to you: you will find him wrapped in swaddling cloths and lying in a manger. But I can see that your baby is not in a feed trough, sir."

"Please, call me Joseph. And my baby *was* in the manger. I made it myself, so I knew there were no sharp edges or places he could get hurt. I filled it with sweet-smelling hay, laid a blanket over it, and placed him in it. But I wanted to bring him out here for a bit to show him to …" Joseph stopped. How could he tell this shepherd that he was showing the baby to His real Father, the LORD Most High?

The shepherd just smiled at him.

"I have a son myself. His name is Caleb. My name is Asher. I remember the night he was born, like it was yesterday. He's thirteen now. I did the same thing as you did the night he was born. I took him outside and introduced him to the Almighty."

The two men stood and grinned at each other. Asher walked over and picked up the lantern. "Can I walk with you back to the house where you're staying? There are about a dozen shepherds running around town looking for your baby. They just want to see the Savior we've been hoping for all these years. That the angels would come to us first, a ragtag band of shepherds, dirty and unclean, and announce God's redemption has been born, well … we can't afford to miss that."

"Yes, yes! Please come. It's not far. I wouldn't take a baby out very far from his mother at night. For one thing, she'd skin me alive if she woke up and found us missing."

"I know exactly what you mean, Joseph."

They went a few feet toward the houses, and then Asher stopped and placed his hand on Joseph's arm.

"Do you suppose I could see him now, before we get back? Just take a peek?"

Joseph looked into the other man's face and examined it for any signs of guile or deceit, but found none. He opened his cloak slightly and shifted the bundle forward. Pulling the blanket back slightly, he let Asher lean in to look.

"He just looks like a baby," Asher thought to himself. *"Like any baby ever born."* To Joseph, he said, "He's a beautiful baby, a handsome boy. I think he takes after you."

Joseph smiled slightly bittersweetly, protecting the secret he had been given regarding the infant in his arms. Covering Jesus again, he told his new friend, "C'mon. It's just up ahead. I think I see some of your other shepherds, too."

"Abba! Did you find him?"

"I did, Caleb. Wait until you see him."

Nathan found his brother while the shepherds went with Joseph inside the house.

"Well, Asher? What does a baby Savior look like?"

"He looks like forgiveness and redemption, Nathan. Come inside and see for yourself."

: : : :

WHEN MARY OPENED HER eyes again, the lower level of Eliana's house was bustling with shepherds, all fussing at each other to be quiet. They weren't facing her, however. They were all facing Joseph, standing like a Roman sentry, his strong arms holding a tiny baby. One voice suddenly stood out over the murmur of the others.

"Caleb? Why are you hugging the wall over there? You need to see this baby. You need to remember this night," Asher called to his young son. There were nearly a dozen shepherds in the lower level of the house.

They all turned as one when Mary croaked dryly, "J-Joseph. Bring me the baby."

The shepherds stepped aside and formed an aisle that Joseph walked carefully along, bringing his wife their baby – *her* baby, he corrected himself. But how could he not think of it as his? He was now responsible for raising this baby boy. It was up to Joseph to teach him the Law, the collective knowledge of the Torah, the books of wisdom, and the prophecies given so many years before. Prophecies about Israel, and prophecies about … this baby he held in his arms.

And then he was handing the child to Mary. He stepped back a half step, leaving a tiny space for the shepherds to file by and look at the baby boy, who was … yawning. Mary pulled her shawl over the two of them and suckled the baby. The shepherds wandered through the lower half of Eliana's house. They looked at the goat and donkey in the stable pen, patting the donkey's flanks and rating the goat as compared with the goats and sheep under their care.

When Mary was done feeding the baby, she called Joseph over. She handed the baby to him and motioned for him to come close. When he leaned in, she said, "Place him in the manger you made. He's well-swaddled in the cloths from Zechariah and Elizabeth, and the manger is new and filled with fresh hay. The shepherds can see him more easily if you do."

Like the good husband he was, Joseph did as his wife told him.

The shepherds gathered around the manger in a rough circle and gazed down at Jesus, all under Joseph's watchful eyes.

Meanwhile, Nathan told Mary about the angels announcing the baby's birth.

"...and so, we just had to come and see him. When an angel tells you to do something, you'd better do it."

Mary gave a small laugh and answered Nathan, "Oh, I know all about angels."

Just then, Eliana came back into the room and announced that it was time to let mother and child rest. Strangely, no one protested. The shepherds began to file out of the door, and Joseph picked up the baby from the feed trough he had made a few days before. Walking toward the bed where Mary lay, he saw the last three shepherds talking in hushed voices in a corner. He saw that it was Asher, his son, Caleb, and Asher's brother, Nathan.

"If you ever need something crafted from wood, you come and find me," Joseph said. "I'm not sure how long we'll stay in Bethlehem, but it'll be for a little while, at least."

Caleb suddenly dashed over and stood before Joseph. He leaned in and spoke softly. Then, turning back momentarily to look over his shoulder at his father and uncle, he hurried out the door to catch up to the rest of the shepherds.

"Nathan," Joseph said, "Don't you want to see the baby? You came all this way in the middle of the night, leaving your flocks behind. Aren't you going to even have a quick look?"

Nathan slowly walked over, his head down, his shepherd's staff in one hand. "The angels said he's the savior. I don't feel like I'm worthy to look at him. I can barely be in his presence."

Joseph looked at the man, knowing how he felt. He had experienced the same feelings of inadequacy when he'd talked with Mary about all the things the angel had told her.

"Nathan," Joseph said again. "Look at him." He pulled the edge of the blanket away from the baby's face. "What do you see?"

Nathan looked, then ducked his head, then looked again. "He's just ... a baby," he said with wonder in his voice.

"Yes, for tonight anyway. Someday, he'll be much more, but for tonight, he's just a baby. But when he grows up, he'll make us more, make us better," Joseph told the shepherd.

Nathan turned and walked to the door where Asher was already waiting. As they went out, Nathan said, "You were right, Asher; he does look like forgiveness."

As the shepherds walked through the streets of Bethlehem, they sang the words the angels had spoken to them, their words echoing between the houses.

"Glory to God in the highest, and on earth peace among men with whom He is pleased."

"But Mary treasured all these things, pondering them in her heart."

Luke 2:19

About This Book

Why I Wrote It

T HE IDEA OF ANOTHER retelling of the Bible or the birth and life of Jesus was probably one of the biggest hurdles to writing this book. The first English-language film portraying the birth of Christ was over a hundred years ago in 1912. Filmed on location in Egypt and Palestine, *From the Manger to the Cross* tells the story of Jesus's life, interspersed with verses from the Bible. And in the twenty-first century, you have the remarkably well-done retelling of Jesus's life in the TV series *The Chosen*.

This book has been coming for a long time, in part because I needed to convince myself that I could write it. It started as a short story focusing on the angel's visit to the Virgin Mary that I wrote around Christmastime in the mid-1990s. That means it took me approximately 28 years to complete this little 150-page book. I can usually get a project of this size done a little quicker these days.

(Forgive me if my timeline is a little wonky; I am going back almost three decades.)

A few years after that short story about the angel's visit to Mary, I added the story of Zechariah in the temple and the angel's visit to the old priest. Then, I set the story aside. A few years passed before I got the urge to add more to the story and inserted the section with Mary's visit to her aunt, Elizabeth. After completing that section, I set it aside again.

Why did I keep setting it aside? The reason's quite simple. The inspiration for this book came from hearing the story, and we don't usually talk about the birth of Jesus and the various events surrounding His birth after January 6 or before November 30. There's a five-week window where the world tolerates the telling of the story of the supernatural birth of the Savior. The world embraces a plethora of movies about fantasy characters and purely fictional stories for Christmas that have nothing to do with the birth of God's Son: *Elf, A Christmas Story, How the Grinch Stole Christmas, Polar Express, National Lampoon's Christmas Vacation, The Nightmare Before Christmas, Home Alone* … need I go on?

Whenever I heard or read the story of Jesus's birth, I was inspired to dig out what I had written, re-read it, and then add to the story. Most years, that left a narrow window for actual writing. Let me explain why.

For much of my younger adult life, the Christmas season was a hectic time of the year *(like it's not for everyone else?).* I was employed in radio for many years and later by a chain of newspapers, two industries that are typically swamped leading up to and during the Christmas season. Eventually, I moved to southeast Georgia and became engaged in full-time church ministry; specifically the music ministry. Christmas is perhaps the busiest time of year there is for retail, advertising, and churches.

For some people, being inundated with the "Christmas Spirit" all day, every day, for six to eight weeks may get them swept up in the "Holiday Season." They catch the spirit. But for me, after years of working in media, I had a tendency to become even less excited about the season when away from my office.

Look at it this way: When you're forced to be joyful, your joy becomes forced and artificial. I could still engage with the true holiday spirit, but it was usually only for brief periods.

Years passed with no changes or additions to the story, but eventually, I dug out what I had started writing nearly three decades ago, buried in a folder labeled SAVE on my computer's hard drive.

Whenever I upgraded or bought a new computer, that folder was transferred. It survived the 2004 trek from northern Minnesota to southeast Georgia when God moved us to a new home with new jobs and responsibilities. Hard drives can come and go, sometimes with disastrous consequences, but I always made sure I had a copy of *The Annunciation* backed up somewhere *(Flash drives were a great invention!)*. There was just *something* about the story that compelled me to keep it and do more with it.

There were times I thought it might be complete: a Christmas short story or novella. I added a title and began editing it under the idea that it was a short story.

The editing process led me to realize I should do some research on Jewish temple practices *(which was good because I had things all wrong!)*. Word to the wise: don't rely on Hollywood movies for historical background. For anything!

I did more research during semester breaks while finishing a Bible degree from 2006-2011. That research convinced me to get rid of the angel's wings *(only the cherubim and seraphim are identified with wings – seraphim in Isaiah 6 and cherubim in Ezekiel 10)*. And these flying creatures are not identified as angels *(What? It's true!)*.

Anytime angels are mentioned other than Gabriel, the archangel Michael, Lucifer, and Abaddon (the Destroyer, who is only mentioned in Revelation 9:1-3,11), they are described as being "like men."

A little more: the Bible doesn't say angels come in two models – no male and female angels like people – and there are no baby angels, toddler or child angels, teenage angels, or elderly angels. God made all the angels at one time at the beginning of creation, and that's all there are, and they ain't no mo. A little biblical research on the subject (no New Age or TV Show-inspired stories), will reveal this truth to you.

After I finished researching angels, I didn't look at the story for a handful of years. It was about 2009 when I wrote the part of the story focused on Joseph after Mary came to see him and she dropped a giant hydrogen bomb in his lap. However, just like numerous times before, when Christmas was over, I put the story away.

The next time I picked it up, I wrote about Joseph's dream and the angel who told him not to be afraid to take Mary as his wife (the angel is not identified). I tried to keep going after Christmas, writing the chapter I titled *Nissuin*, which can be loosely translated as married life, but my plate was running over. I was the director of the music department at my church, and I also had the completion of my college degree in my sights. So, I tucked the book away for another time and graduated *summa cum laude* in 2011. I added Senior Adult

Ministry responsibilities at church, and *The Annunciation* went on the back burner again, this time for almost a decade.

At the end of 2020, I stepped away from full-time church ministry after twelve years at First Baptist Church, St. Marys, GA. In 2021, at age 64, looking for something I could carry with me into retirement, I became a freelance editor, proofreader, and ghostwriter. It wasn't long before "author" was added to that list.

I dusted off my old blog and put some new stories up. I reworked some of my old, old(!) stories, letting people read them for the first time in decades *(Yes, I was blogging back in the mid-90s before it was cool!)*. And then one day, I saw it.

It was hiding inside a folder buried in my Documents folder: *The Annunciation*. It was like seeing an old friend for the first time in years.

I digitally blew the dust off, read through it, made some edits, trimmed some fluff, took one part – Joseph's story – and posted it on my blog at Christmastime. I've always felt Joseph doesn't get enough credit in the Bible. I know the Bible gives him the credit God wanted him to have, but I wanted to know more about his story. I am a father and a husband, and I can empathize with Joseph's emotions and heartbreak.

When I pulled the manuscript out of hiding again in 2023, Joseph's story was one of the first things I wanted to work on. I had decided I was actually going to do something with the story. First, though, I had to fix some things in Zechariah's story, another man who, like Joseph, came to fatherhood in an unexpected way.

Once Joseph and Mary were hitched, I thought I was done, but my fingers kept going. For the first time in years, I added some characters and their viewpoints and experiences to the story. I wanted to know more about that night when Jesus was born and about the shepherds who came to see the baby after the angels announced His birth.

I wrote the shepherds' story and brought them to Bethlehem like the angel said they should. Once in the City of David, they discovered Joseph introducing Jesus to His true Father (one of the fictional additions to the story).

Something else I discovered: everyone back then (the first century) would have known that Jesus wasn't Joseph's biological son because the tradition at the time was to name the firstborn son after the father. If Joseph and Mary had followed tradition, Jesus should have been Joseph Josephson (technically Jesus bar Joseph – bar means 'son of'), but He was named after His real Father.

---

*"Behold, the virgin shall be with child and shall
bear a Son, and they shall call His name
Immanuel," which translated means,
"God with us."*

Matthew 1:23

When I finished writing the shepherds' story, it finally felt complete. I didn't feel like I needed to go to the temple on the eighth day with Mary and Joseph to see old Simeon and Anna, the prophetess, waiting for the Messiah. I didn't feel like I needed to bring the magi into the story. They didn't show up until Jesus was somewhere between six months and two years old.

(All the Christmas scenes showing the little family, the shepherds, and the three wise men are incorrect. You know that, right? And you know a manger is a feed trough, not the stable, right?)

So, now it's done. It's out of my hands and into yours. This book is intended to help you recapture the wonder and awe of Christmas that may have slipped out of your grasp due to the commercialization of the season. Christmas should fill you with amazement and reverence. I want you to get "the feels" again, but for the true story, not the elf on the shelf, Rudolph, Frosty, Ralph, or any of the others.

I want you to read this story and think about how these real people felt and how you would feel in their places. I want you to feel their frustration, wonder, anger, worship, and amazement over the extent to which God was willing to go to bring us back into a right relationship with Him. We couldn't do it ourselves, so He paid our fare.

Warning: big letters ahead.

DISCLAIMER: THIS BOOK IS NOT THE INSPIRED WORD OF GOD.

It is a fictionalized treatment of the events surrounding Jesus's birth. Although it contains selected passages from the Bible, it is <u>biblical</u> <u>historical</u> <u>fiction</u>. So, please don't come after me with pitchforks and torches!

Also, there are a bunch of things in my story that are made up. We can't know about them for sure because the Bible doesn't tell us *(that was the whole point of writing this book in the first place!).*

Some early readers have thought I made the characters too modern, but people being people and the fact that we haven't changed very much in over 2000 years means I could be right on the nose with some of my portrayals. I could also be way out in left field somewhere. The good news so far is I haven't been struck down by lightning.

Disclaimer: There is no archaeological or scientific evidence for some of the props I have used. I particular, the idea that the swaddling cloths were a gift from Zechariah and Elizabeth is a pure Hallmark-style movie scene. It's a great idea, but there is no evidence for that whatsoever, so don't make it part of your Christmas Eve celebration. It has been suggested over the years, but historians and archeologists have never found a shred of supportive evidence. When someone finds a letter from Zechariah and Elizabeth saying they hope Mary and Joseph appreciated the special swaddling cloths they gave them, *then* we can say we have justification for it.

Eddie Arthur, a Bible translator with Wycliffe, has stated that there are a number of problems with the traditional Christmas story interpretation we have handed down through the years. He says we should apologize to the women of Bethlehem for believing they neglected Mary and Joseph in their hour of need.

He wrote: "Mary and Joseph were almost certainly not condemned to sleep in a cattle shed by a heartless innkeeper. Joseph's family was from Bethlehem; he had relatives there who would certainly have put him up. However, because there was no space in the guest room (wrongly translated as "inn" in many English translations), Mary and

Joseph had to sleep in the downstairs space that some of the family shared with the animals. A strange setting to us, maybe, but not at all unusual in the context.

"The local women would have rallied round to support her, and there would be experienced midwives there to advise Mary and help out when needed. It wasn't a modern-day hospital with formally trained staff, but these women would have seen lots of babies born, and they knew what to do. Meanwhile, Joseph, as a mere, useless male, would have been dispatched somewhere out of the way, probably to share some wine with the local men who would tell stories about the births of their children."

"We read the story of the Nativity from the point of view of our individualistic society, and we read into it on the basis of our own experience. The problem is that the Bible was written long ago in a country far, far away. We need to read and understand the Bible in its own context before applying it to ours."

(If you'd like to read more, follow the link. Eddie Arthur, Kouya.net, Eddie and Sue Arthur's blog https://www.kouya.net/?p=8779)

So, now you know *how* I wrote this small book, and can maybe figure out I wrote it, too. Christmas should be and can be a wondrous, awe-inspiring time of year. God's plan to give us mercy and grace had finally reached its time; it had "ripened," if you will. Rather like Mary when they were in Bethlehem: *"While they were there, the days were completed for her to give birth"* (Luke 2:6).

God knew how He was going to rescue us since before we needed rescuing, way back before the Garden of Eden. *"He chose us in Him before the foundation of the world, that we would be holy and blameless before Him"* (Ephesians 1:4).

"All who dwell on the earth will worship him, everyone whose name has not been written from the foundation of the world in the book of life of the Lamb who has been slain" (Revelation 13:8).

The stories of Creation, the patriarchs, and even the story of Jesus's birth were originally passed on orally by storytellers. I like to think that some first-century storytellers—maybe shepherds or their descendants—told their children about the night the angels announced the birth of the Savior of the world to a bunch of stinky shepherds watching their sheep in the fields around Bethlehem. And I like to think they made the story come alive for their children, not just giving them a barebones outline.

If you'd like to share my book with your children, I'd love to hear from you about how you've done so. Drop me an email at

mkzpublishing@gmail.com

Oh, yeah. One more thing. If you like this book, leave a rating and review where you got it at amazon.com (https://www.amazon.com/dp/B0DDH3FK47) or on goodreads.com.

About the Author

MICHAEL K. ZIMMERLI IS a freelance author, editor, and proofreader. He has helped dozens of people around the world become published authors since embarking on this journey in 2021.

He is the author of The Blue Bridge Mysteries, a series of clean, light mysteries set in northeast Florida and southeast Georgia. In the stories, Jimmy Favreaux, Wendi Lyst, her father-in-law Hillary Lyst, and Robert (Pepé) Perez work together to solve murders and other crimes. Book #4, *Perchance 2 Dream*, was published in 2024. Jimmy, a private investigator, lives within rock-throwing distance of the famous Highway 17 Blue Bridge across the Saint Marys River, which marks the Florida–Georgia border.

Mike worked in radio for almost twenty years, newspapers and IT for a half-dozen more, and full-time ministry for nearly seventeen. He still has many stories to tell. In addition to the *Blue Bridge Mysteries* and *The Annunciation*, he's been kicking around the idea of writing a biblical historical fiction account of the Apostle Paul, Timothy, and Silas on one of Paul's missionary journeys.

Michael is the father of two and the husband of one. Mike and Mary Zimmerli have been married since 1980. He is a Senior Adult Sunday School class teacher, deacon, and musician.

If you skipped the previous section, please let me know if you like this fictional treatment of biblical history.

Send me an email at
mkzpublishing@gmail.com
or leave me a review on Amazon or Goodreads.
Reviews are very important to independent authors.